Saying Good-bye to London

Saying Good-bye to London

JULIE BURTINSHAW

Second Story Press

Library and Archives Canada Cataloguing in Publication

Burtinshaw, Julie, 1958-, author
Saying good-bye to London / by Julie Burtinshaw.

Issued in print and electronic formats.
ISBN 978-1-77260-029-2 (paperback).
—ISBN 978-1-77260-030-8 (epub)

I. Title.

PS8553.U69623S29 2017   jC813'.6   C2016-907246-0

C2016-907353-X

Cover illustration © Katy Dockrill, i2iart.com

Edited by Kathryn Cole, Carolyn Jackson
Copyedited by Kelly Jones
Design by Melissa Kaita

Printed and bound in Canada

Second Story Press gratefully acknowledges the support of the
Ontario Arts Council and the Canada Council for the Arts for our
publishing program. We acknowledge the financial support of the
Government of Canada through the Canada Book Fund.

ONTARIO ARTS COUNCIL
CONSEIL DES ARTS DE L'ONTARIO
an Ontario government agency
un organisme du gouvernement de l'Ontario

Canada Council   Conseil des Arts
for the Arts   du Canada

Funded by the Government of Canada
Financé par le gouvernement du Canada

 Canadä

Published by
SECOND STORY PRESS
20 Maud Street, Suite 401
Toronto, ON M5V 2M5
www.secondstorypress.ca

This book is dedicated to future adults.
Imagine all you can do.

*It's not what happens to you but
how you react to it that matters.*
                                    —Epictetus

Prologue

Francis Sloan didn't want to go to the dance. Girls scared him. Gaming seemed the better, safer option on a sweltering August night. "No way," he'd griped, but despite his protests, Kevin, his best friend, had cajoled him into it.

"You never know. You might meet someone. It's better than a school dance, because they'll be kids from all over."

"Yeah, right." At fifteen, Francis, shy despite his lanky frame and gray-blue eyes, didn't see much chance of that *ever* happening, but he'd gone along because his best friend asked— no, begged—him to.

And lately, Kevin hadn't wanted to do much of anything. Not since his dad's diagnosis a few months earlier. You didn't have to be an oncologist to know that Kevin's dad didn't have much to be optimistic about—anybody could see that. His sunken cheeks, his wasted body, and his wispy hair all pointed to a future battle lost. Still, he hadn't lost the light in his eyes. Not like Kevin.

So Francis agreed. When they got to the dance, it was in full swing. The thumping music and swaying bodies didn't help Francis's awkwardness. He planted himself in the darkest corner of the gym with the other petrified boys, folded his arms across his chest, put on his best bored expression, and fiddled with his phone. Every so often, when it felt safe, he lifted his hazy eyes to sneak a look at the line of girls against the opposite wall. It would be simpler to leap across Niagara Falls than to take the thirty steps needed to close the distance between them.

Kevin, always in tune with Francis's thoughts, interrupted his brooding with a friendly elbow jab. "Drink?" He pushed a small silver container into his hand.

Francis accepted the flask gratefully. "How'd you get this by the bag check?" He took a swig, and the fiery liquid warmed his throat.

Kevin shrugged off his friend's admiration. "That's the beauty of flasks that double as belt buckles," he said nonchalantly, taking a long appreciative drink. "There's not a lot there, but it's strong stuff."

They emptied the flask between them, and within minutes, Francis felt like he could breathe again. So when the tall, intriguing girl with the heavy, black eyeliner and arching brows appeared out of the dense vapor of the fog machine, he managed to return her defiant look and keep his knees from buckling.

"Hi," she said, twirling a strand of dark hair in her fingers.

"Hi," he muttered. Then, more strongly: "Hello."

Her eyes softened, and she laughed.

He smiled. But when she asked him to dance, he thought to himself, *Are you kidding?*

"Sure," he said, as if this kind of thing happened to him every day.

"I'm Sawyer." She eyeballed him until he mumbled his name, and then she smiled boldly. "Come on." She took his hand and pulled him out onto the floor, where they danced under the rainbow lights until the DJ had spun his last record.

By then, Francis felt a foot taller. With confidence he didn't know he possessed, he pulled Sawyer into a long kiss.

"I think we're going to be seeing a lot of each other," she whispered.

Francis smiled. "I hope so." He wondered if she could hear his heart pounding over the tremble in his voice. What could a girl like her possibly see in a boy like him?

"Hey, let's go outside," she said. "You know, get some air."

He would have gone anywhere with her. He took her extended hand and followed her outside. She skirted the groups of kids drinking and talking and led him to a quiet spot where they could be alone.

He was too caught up in the moment to think about what would happen next and how it might change his life forever. It would have been nice to stand outside the community center and kiss her all night, but Kevin appeared, and his irritating throat-clearing and foot-shuffling made that impossible.

He understood Kevin's impatience. It hadn't been easy to

talk their parents into letting them walk home, even though they lived only a few blocks away. If they were late, there would be trouble.

"Seems like your friend is trying to tell you something," Sawyer whispered, an underlying touch of humor in her voice. She pushed him away gently. "See you soon, Francis Sloan."

He watched her until she disappeared from his sight, then he remembered to say good-bye. "See you," he murmured to her departing figure, savoring the taste of her on his lips.

He did his best to pull himself together before he joined his friend. "I told you you'd meet someone," Kevin said with satisfaction as they walked home from the dance. "Did you get her number?"

Francis nodded. "Better. We're going to see each other tomorrow."

Kevin let out a whoop and high-fived Francis. "Beats a night of Call of Duty! So you guys have an actual date?"

"Sort of. Her mom isn't always around, so I'm going to her place."

"Maybe you'll get lucky." Kevin poked Francis in the ribs. He winked, but Francis knew he felt out of his depth. No wonder—this wasn't familiar territory—neither of them had been with a girl before. In truth, the whole thing seemed impossible. Still…

"Huh. I wish." Francis laughed. "She's pretty hot."

Kevin rubbed his hands together and whistled softly. "Yeah."

"What about you?" Francis changed the subject, trying not

to be too obvious about it. "I saw you dancing with a hottie. Did you get her number?"

"Yeah, but she got drunk and left before the dance ended, so no luck."

Francis laughed. He wasn't ready to talk about his feelings, and besides, he didn't want to disrespect Sawyer, even in fun, even with Kevin. "She's older," he said. "Sixteen. She goes to public school and lives on the other side of town. She's had a boyfriend too, so she's experienced." He could still taste her lips on his and feel her soft skin beneath his hands.

Kevin rolled his eyes. "She's kind of emo."

"She's beautiful," Francis said with a sigh. "And she's not emo—she just has her own style. She's just, well…she's Sawyer."

"Man," Kevin said, "you've got it bad." He shoved his hands into his jean pockets and scowled, signaling the end of the conversation. "So I guess I won't be seeing you tomorrow afternoon." It was a statement not a question, and it was true, so Francis didn't bother to answer.

They cut through the wooded park that bordered their neighborhood, each lost in his own thoughts. It was dark, past midnight, and the air had cooled. Except for the sound of the light breeze in the trees and their breathing, it was quiet. A sliver of moonlight lit the path, but they could have found their way home blindfolded. They'd grown up in this area, and they knew by heart each tree and the narrow trails that wound between them.

The closer the boys got to Kevin's house, the quieter and smaller Kevin became. His broad shoulders slumped, and his head dropped until his curly blond hair created a veil of protection over his large, sad eyes.

Francis wished it were different. The last six months with Kevin had been difficult. Witnessing his friend suffer through his dad's illness had been like watching a candle slowly sputter out. Francis felt powerless, guilty. He'd had a blast at the dance; he'd met a girl. He'd kissed that girl and she'd kissed him back. He couldn't wait for tomorrow afternoon. But Kevin had struck out.

He'd blown off Kevin at the dance without giving it a thought.

They arrived at Kevin's house first. Except for one room on the ground floor, all the lights were off in the stately Elizabethan-style home. "Your dad's up," Francis noted. They'd converted the den into a sickroom when Mr. Croyden could no longer manage the stairs. There was a hospital bed, and the smell of sickness permeated the once comfortable study. Books still lined the walls, but the desk and soft leather chairs had been removed, the carpets drawn back, and a big flat-screen TV stuck hurriedly on a wall that had once boasted colorful paintings. In the middle of it all, Mr. Croyden slowly expired, all the while doing his best to make everyone feel better—especially his son.

"Yeah. He wakes up for more pain drugs."

They stood in awkward silence for a few seconds before Kevin turned up the path to his front door. "See you." His body language spoke for itself.

"Hey," Francis called after him. "Thanks for making me go tonight." And, almost as an afterthought, because Sawyer occupied his thoughts, he said, "Say hi to your dad for me."

Kevin looked away, his voice barely audible. "Yeah. Whatever. Have a good time tomorrow."

"Thanks," Francis replied. "I'll catch you later."

Kevin paused on the stoop, then he ducked inside and the door swung shut behind him.

• • •

In the two weeks before the start of school, "later" never happened. Francis went to see Sawyer the next day and the day after that and the day after that. Because she lived on the East Side, and Francis on the West Side of Vancouver, the meet-ups weren't easy—a forty-minute bus ride for Francis—but he'd have made the trek if it had been three times as long. He got into the habit of catching up on his summer reading assignment on the bus. He'd text Sawyer as he approached her stop, and she'd be waiting for him when he got off the bus.

At first he felt shy when around her, but by their third date, they'd become inseparable. Francis was a willing tourist in a part of the city he'd never known. Sawyer enjoyed taking him into the small galleries, music stores, and coffee shops that lined the busy street she lived on. "How long have you lived here?" she inquired incredulously, when Francis finally admitted that he'd never set foot on Main Street.

"Well, it's a long way from my place," he defended, wondering why he'd missed out on such a vibrant part of the city. "Anyway, I'm here now."

On warm days, she'd take him to small, heavily treed parks, and they would sit with their arms around each other, kissing and talking in their own world.

On their fifth day together, Sawyer was waiting impatiently at the bus stop for Francis. As soon as his feet hit the sidewalk, she grabbed his hand. "I've been waiting for ages. Come on. Follow me."

She hurried down the street, not slowing her pace until they arrived in front of a tall, blue-and-white, three-story Victorian house with a steep, wide staircase leading to the entrance. Six mailboxes lined the doorframe. "Here we are," she said, climbing the stairs and pushing open the front door. "My house." She grinned. "Mom won't be home for hours."

Francis's stomach did a slow flip, and, for a split second, he hesitated. He blinked. So what?

He followed her inside. It didn't matter. Nothing mattered, except for the thought of Sawyer's slim, naked body and inviting smile.

Then the impossible happened, and Francis felt the gulf between his old self and his new self widen.

Part One

How frail the human heart must be—a throbbing pulse, a trembling thing—a fragile, shining instrument of crystal, which can either weep, or sing.

—Sylvia Plath

Chapter One

The Sloan house possessed a muted sense of quiet, like a private library, but Sawyer couldn't have known this when she slammed the front door shut behind them with a thunderous bang. In the apartment she shared with her mother, there were very few rules.

Francis, who had been raised to close doors softly so as not to wake his little brothers, jumped at the thud of wood striking wood. Already feeling tightly wound, he turned on her. "Shit, Sawyer. Go easy on the door!"

The loud noise reverberated through the front hall, announcing their arrival, even though Francis had made sure everybody would be out. It was bad enough bringing his girl-friend over; he couldn't fathom a parental introduction. Sawyer, as he'd planned, was sure this would be the day she finally got to meet his family, and that was fine with him. It's what he needed her to believe.

But a sound from deep inside the house stopped Francis cold in his tracks. Had he imagined it?

Sawyer, close on his heels, bumped into him and swore under her breath. "Jesus, Francis. What's with you?" Raising her voice, she scolded, "I'm here to meet your mom, not Medusa."

Her grade eleven class had been studying Greek mythology and she liked to sprinkle her conversation with mythological figures. "Is she like Medusa?"

"Medusa?" Francis rolled his eyes. "You know, most of the time, I don't know what or who you're talking about."

She gave him a funny look. "You seem kind of distracted. Medusa. You know, Gorgon monster, ringlets made of poisonous snakes. One look and you turn to stone. That *Medusa*."

She sighed as if this were common knowledge and shrugged off her book-laden backpack. It fell to the floor with a solid thump. Francis winced.

In the few weeks he'd known her, he'd never seen Sawyer do anything quietly. *Most* of the time, he liked that about her— not now, though.

Why had he agreed to this? Because he found it impossible to say no to her. Because she'd keep bugging him until he agreed.

"You can't keep putting me off. I want to meet your family."

So here they were. Francis felt self-conscious about his neighborhood. He felt even more uncomfortable about his house. Today, against the backdrop of a sky the color of concrete, the soft light from the chandelier above them lent the front hall an elegant air. Outside, towering oak trees lined the wide streets like sentries, guarding against non-pedigreed intruders. Sawyer, he guessed, would have a lot to say about all of this later.

"Pretty swank" had been her only comment when they'd turned onto his winding street minutes earlier.

Now she stood in his front hall, twirling her hair irritably, while he removed his shoes and tucked them into the shoe rack. Next, he took off his backpack and hung it on a hook on the wall, and then he did the same with his coat. Sawyer was impatient.

"Come on, Francis! Let's go and meet your clan. In a house this size, we might have to send out a search party."

He couldn't tell if her sarcasm was meant to criticize or amuse.

"Very funny," he said. "Actually, I don't think anyone is home, even though I told them to be." The lie rolled easily off his tongue. "Mom never said a word about going out."

He rearranged his face into disappointment, which became the real thing as a musical giggle floated down the hall.

"No way," he muttered as a second burst of laughter reached his ears.

In that second, he grasped the full extent of his miscalculation. What if they simply retraced their footsteps and slipped quietly back into the safety and anonymity of the street?

He skidded to a stop. "I can't do this."

Sawyer gave him a little push from behind. "What's that noise?"

"Well, let's just say I don't think you have to worry about *us* finding *them*." The clomp-drag of heavy, uneven footsteps came from down the hall. Too late to run for it.

"Oh god." He turned terrified eyes on Sawyer. "They're home!"

She gave him a puzzled look. "What's up with you today?"

"Wait for it." He held up his hand. "Here they come." On cue, his mom appeared at the end of the long hallway.

"Hi," Francis managed, trying to see her through Sawyer's eyes. She was tall, like him, the same blue-gray eyes, hers framed by laugh lines. She lurched like a wounded giant to the left and the right, her balance compromised by the twin five-year-old boys who clung to her like monkeys, one on each leg.

"Gosh," exclaimed Sawyer, eyeing the scene before her.

The little boys were ridiculously cute, with dark skin, curly hair, solemn faces, and large, brown eyes, while their mother was white, about five-foot-eight, with a halo of curly red hair. She wore designer jeans and a black T-shirt that shouted "Pipe Up against Oil Pipelines."

All three were covered in a light dusting of flour. When Sawyer saw them, she burst into delighted laughter.

Francis's mom tried, but failed, to shake off the boys.

"I give up," she said with a laugh, beaming at Sawyer. "Goodness, did you compare me to Medusa just now? Francis, what have you been saying about me? And who is your charming friend with a love of Greek mythology? You didn't tell me you'd be bringing a guest home after school."

"Yes, I did," he mumbled. "At least, I thought I did."

His mom gave him "the look" and brushed a strand of hair off her cheek, unable to hide her astonishment at seeing her son with a girl in tow, a pretty girl—despite her raccoon eyes and cherry-red lips. Francis wasn't fooled by his mother's subterfuge. Her surprised expression reminded him of the big-eyed bullfrog he'd netted in the backyard pond for his young brothers.

"The Medusa thing was just a joke," Sawyer explained. "I mean, I was teasing Francis. No offense meant."

"None taken."

Francis cleared his throat. "I kind of like Medusa," he said, regaining his composure. "It suits you, Mom—especially when you don't brush your hair."

His mom shot him a withering look. "Very funny. Now, introductions please, Francis."

"I'm getting to that. Sawyer, this is my mom, and the kid on her left leg is Nate. The one on her right is Devon. Mom, this is Sawyer Martin."

His mom grinned, attempted to shake the twins off her legs once again, then gave up and turned to Sawyer. "Nice to meet you. I'd shake your hand, but as you can see, we've been baking, and I'm covered in flour and kids." She held up her hands as unnecessary proof.

Nate pointed at Sawyer. "Is she your girlfriend?" Carefully, he unlatched himself from his mother's leg and took a tentative step forward. He squatted in front of the new arrival, his eyes fixed on the bright purple toenail that protruded from a gaping hole in Sawyer's striped sock. He gazed up at her with enormous brown eyes. "If you and Francis are in love, does that mean you kiss?"

"Do you kiss?" Devon mimicked, sidling up beside his brother. They both puckered up their lips.

Francis looked at his mom, his eyes pleading.

She shrugged. "It's a valid question, honey. I'm quite grateful to them for asking it."

"Shut up, you two," he cautioned the twins, his face a deep red. "Stop being rude, or you're going to be in big trouble."

The boys collapsed onto the floor in a puddle of giggles.

Sawyer, unfazed, crouched down to their level. "God, how do you tell them apart? I'll kiss *you* if you're not careful." She made a grab for the boys' plump legs. They got up and ran screaming and laughing down the hall.

"Yuck! Girl germs!" they called out. "Girl germs!"

Sawyer made to go after them, but Francis held her back. "You'll just encourage them," he cautioned. "Then they'll be crazier than usual."

"I'm coming for you," Sawyer shouted after them, ignoring him. "At some point."

"Oh, very effective." His mom laughed. "I think they like you, Sawyer. Anyway, welcome to our chaos. Make yourself at home, and"—turning to Francis—"I assume you'll visit on the main floor. No going upstairs." She gave him a warning look, not lost on Sawyer.

"Don't worry," Sawyer said, turning to her with mock seriousness. "We're not likely to sneak up to Francis's bedroom for a quick make-out session. I want to impress you on our first meeting, not get kicked out of your house!"

Francis's cheeks burned. "She thinks she's funny." He

glared at Sawyer. "She's not. Come on. We'll grab something to eat, then take Ralph for a"—he lowered his voice to a whisper—"*w-a-l-k*."

"Who's Ralph?" Sawyer said and looked around suspiciously. "Another gorgeous brother? Why does he need a walk?"

"Oh no," Francis's mother groaned. "Now you've done it. We don't say that word out loud in our house."

"*Walk*?" Sawyer looked puzzled.

"Shhh," Francis warned.

"Too late," his mom said with a sigh. "Here he comes."

A loud bark emanated from deep inside the house, followed by excited yips. Then a huge yellow Lab skated around the corner, slipping and sliding on the hardwood floor. The dog skidded to a messy stop at Sawyer's feet. He pushed his nose into her hand. "*Woof, woof, woof.*"

"You have a dog, Francis! And he smells like cookie dough! You never told me. I love dogs, especially dogs that understand English. Walk. You want a walk?" She rubbed his ears and kissed the top of his head. "He's so soft."

"Sawyer, meet Ralph." With luck, the visit would be over before it started. Ralph was the excuse Francis needed to escape. He reached for the leash that hung on a hook beside the front door. "And now that you've said *walk*, we have to go right away or he'll never leave us alone. See you later, Mom." He opened the door.

"Don't be rude, Francis. Have a snack first," admonished his mother. "Ralph will be fine. Why don't you two go to the living room and I'll round up something to tide you over until dinner?"

"Sounds great. Thanks, Mrs. S. I'm starving!" Sawyer rubbed her hands together.

"Not for long," his mother said, laughing, and hurried down the hall.

When she was gone, Sawyer turned to Francis. "Nice digs." She eyed the paintings that lined the walls. "I don't know why you were so uptight about showing those off."

Francis looked at Sawyer. "The thing is, I'd rather be at your place." He started toward the living room, Sawyer on his heels.

"Well, too bad. I think I like it better here." She looked around, taking in the large, comfortable space, the green velvet curtains, woven Indian rugs, worn oak floor, and African tribal face masks.

"Wow. Fancy! There's stuff here from all over the world. *Who is that?*" She pointed at a fat tabby cat curled up on the leather couch.

"That's Steve."

"Weird name for a cat." She scooped the cat up, pulled him onto her knee, and sank into the soft cushions.

"He's a weird cat."

"Sit," she ordered Francis while scratching Steve's head. He purred happily.

"A friend for life," Francis commented, obeying her but sitting down at the opposite end of the couch. He put as much space between them as he could. Then, changing the subject, he said, "This is bizarre." He immediately stood up. "Should I put some music on?"

"Sure. You've got enough vinyl and CDs in here to open a store."

"I guess." He picked up the iPod attached to the speaker system and hit play. "Let's take a chance on the music."

Sawyer giggled when the sentimental "Open Arms" by Journey came on.

"Sorry." Francis turned the volume down and hastily explained the song choice to Sawyer. "My mom's music."

She smiled. "A love song. Sweet. Are you trying to tell me something?" She fluttered eyelashes in mock seduction.

"Uh, I guess…" He bit his top lip. "Like, can we go now? Oh no," he added.

"What's that?" asked Sawyer, putting her finger to her lips. "Can you hear it? A sort of wailing."

"That," Francis said with a sigh, "is Mom. She loves to sing, but she's tone-deaf. Cover your ears."

Sawyer giggled. "Your mom is cool."

In spite of his unease, Francis couldn't help but laugh as his mother struggled to hit a high note. He rolled his eyes. "She's never been able to carry a tune."

"Ten points for trying," Sawyer said, picking up the blue-and-yellow cushion beside her and running her hand over it. "Hand-embroidered silk. You're rich," she stated matter-of-factly. "Everyone in this whole neighborhood is rich. No wonder you never made it across town."

Francis got up and changed the song, ignoring her; there was no point in starting an argument he'd never win. When he returned to the couch, he sat a few inches closer to Sawyer.

"Like I said before, it's relative, isn't it? You should see some of the boys in my school."

"You never told me about your brothers. You know, that they are…"

"Adopted."

"Well, I was going to say black, but adopted, yeah."

"It didn't seem important. They're just my pesky, adorable brothers." Francis's eyes wandered to the African art that filled the room. "They were three months old when we got them. They were born in the Ivory Coast—in Africa," he added as an afterthought.

"I know where the Ivory Coast is. Even public school kids learn geography, Francis."

"I didn't mean it that way." That was exactly why he hadn't wanted to bring her here to his home. He knew she'd put him under a microscope and that she wouldn't like what she saw.

"That's how it sounded to me. Anyway," she continued, "what happened to their real parents?"

"Birth parents," Francis corrected. "We're their *real* family." He paused. "It's sad. We don't know anything about their dad, but their mom was killed in cross fire in the civil war."

"Poor little guys."

"They're actually pretty happy little guys," he said. "They don't need your sympathy."

"Sorry," Sawyer murmured. "Touchy." She picked at the cushion again and put it protectively over her stomach. "Go on."

"They were newborns when they were left at the orphanage," Francis continued. "They don't remember a thing about those days. It's hard to talk about. I mean, someone's misfortune was our fortune."

Sawyer nodded. "So that explains all the African stuff around here. Don't beat yourself up. They're lucky to have you now." She patted the cushion beside her. "Come closer. I don't bite. Unless, of course…" She stuck her tongue out and licked her lips slowly.

"Sawyer, stop it! My mom could walk in any second."

"Relax, Francis. It's not illegal to have a girlfriend."

On cue, his mom arrived, carrying a tray laden with sandwiches, cookies, and two tall glasses of iced tea. "It certainly isn't," she joked. "But it's new for us. Francis has never brought a girl home before."

"Mom!"

His mother winked at him. He prayed she'd make a quick exit, but instead she turned her attention to Sawyer. "What an interesting name you have."

"My mom named me Sawyer after Tom Sawyer. My grandfather used to read it to her when she was a kid, but he died when she was ten, so she named me Sawyer because she said those were good days."

"Hmm, and what school do you go to, Sawyer?"

"Third degree," Francis grumbled, biting into a cookie.

"Well, you don't meet many girls, going to an all-boys school. I'm just curious. Do you go to Townsend?" she asked.

Townsend was the all-girls school.

Sawyer picked a sandwich from the tray and took a big bite. "Yummy. No. No private school for me. I go to Robert Service Secondary."

Francis's mom cocked her head to one side. "I'm not familiar with that school."

"East Side," Sawyer clarified. "You wouldn't know it. It's not famous for much, except we have a great breakfast and lunch program for the little kids."

Francis saw the twinkle in his girlfriend's eye and the wheels turning in his mother's brain. She didn't have a clue what Sawyer meant.

"Oh. That's nice." Confirming his suspicion, she continued with a smile. "Francis likes a hot lunch, but that's a Friday treat. I like to send him to school with a lunch I've made. That way I know he is eating healthy food and not junk."

"How sweet," Sawyer purred. "But it's not quite the same thing."

Francis looked to see if his mom detected the sarcasm, but her bewildered expression painted a firm no.

"Anyway," Sawyer went on, "we moved here from London last year."

"London." His mother perked up. "We've been there several times, haven't we, Francis? Lovely city. I can't get enough of the Tate Modern, although my family has certainly never appreciated it. They like to spend their time digging through record stores and going to plays and concerts."

"I meant London, Ontario," Sawyer clarified. "Not quite as exciting. But I loved it there," she added wistfully.

"Oh. Well, I'm sure it's a lovely place, in its own way. A bit cold, though." His mother spoke through pursed lips and brushed some flour off her sleeve. "How did you two meet?"

"We should take Ralph for his walk," Francis interjected. "Now."

They both ignored him. He picked up a sandwich and paced around the room, keeping an eye on them from a distance. Sawyer and his mother were polar opposites in every way, but they had a lot to say to each other. In fact, Sawyer couldn't seem to shut up.

"To answer your question, Francis and I met at a dance." She helped herself to three cookies, offering one to Ralph, who greedily swallowed it in one gulp, then stared at her in adoration.

"Not a great idea." His mom shook her head. "He's fat enough as it is. Iced tea?"

"Yes. Please."

"So you met at a dance? Really? At school?" She picked up one of the two tall glasses on the tray. "Mmm," she said, sipping on Francis's iced tea. She handed the other glass to Sawyer. "Cheers."

"Thank you." Sawyer took a sip. "No, we met at the community center—the one in this 'hood. Your son has some terrific moves on the dance floor."

"Oh, spare me," Francis muttered, his comment falling on deaf ears.

"He does, does he? Must have picked them up from me. When he was a little boy, I used to turn the music on full blast and we'd dance until we dropped." She smiled at the memory. "The twins love to dance too."

Francis stuffed another sandwich into his mouth. It tasted like gravel, but it gave him the excuse he needed to avoid talking.

Why couldn't Sawyer just stop blabbing? But no. She had to describe the night they met—and to his mother of all people.

"And after that, we started hanging together. That was over a month and a half ago—actually, six weeks and one day—so I said, 'Time to meet the family!' and here we are. Right, Francis?"

Francis scowled at Sawyer. She scowled right back at him. "Anything you'd care to add?"

"I wasn't listening."

"Don't mind him," his mother said. "He's always been a bit of a dreamer." She swirled the ice around in her empty glass and stood up. "Francis, I'm afraid I've drunk your iced tea. Would you like one?"

"No, thanks."

"Sawyer, another one?"

"Sure, that would be nice," Sawyer replied. "I'm not used to being waited on."

Francis shook his head. "I seriously think we should get going."

"Okay," Sawyer snapped, and dumped Steve unceremoniously onto the floor. The cat's withering look was lost on her. "Since you can't relax, let's go."

She jumped up and grabbed Francis's hand. It was an intimate gesture. "Come on." She pulled him toward the hallway.

His mother raised her eyebrows, but he daren't shake Sawyer off. She'd be furious. She'd take it the wrong way and assume he was ashamed of her. He'd learned over the last six weeks that she had a short fuse.

"It's probably better if I skip the iced tea, anyway. My stomach's been a bit upset lately, so I probably shouldn't load up on sugar."

His mom shook her head. "I hope it's not the flu. The twins were sick with the flu for a week and it was horrible, for all of us."

"I don't know," Sawyer replied. "School's stressful right now. Lots of homework. Lots of late nights." She dropped Francis's hand and took hold of his arm. "I think I got up too quickly."

"You've gone a bit white," said his mom. "Sit back down, take a deep breath, and the nausea will fade."

"Actually, may I use your bathroom?"

"I'll show you the way." She touched Sawyer gently on her arm. "Are you sure you're up for a walk with a crazy pooch?"

Francis watched the color slowly return to his girlfriend's face. She nodded. "You're very kind…I think the fresh air might help me feel better."

"Meet you in the front yard." Francis attached Ralph's leash to the dog's collar and escaped out the door. They waited impatiently outside until Sawyer and his mom reappeared. Sawyer seemed much better.

"Thanks for the snacks, Mrs. S, and the iced tea. I hope Francis invites me over again," she called cheerfully as she tied up the laces on her vivid pink Converse.

Kevin's mom smiled. "It was nice meeting you, Sawyer," she said. "Get some rest. You don't want to get sick. I hope you'll come back soon."

Was it his imagination, or did Francis hear a level of doubt in his mother's voice? Screw it. He pushed the thought away. After all, it wasn't up to his mom to choose his girlfriend.

Chapter Two

Once away from home, his mother's curious eyes, and his brothers' saucy comments, Francis relaxed. When Sawyer pressed her hand into his, he squeezed her fingers affectionately. They made their way toward the park in happy silence. Ralph pulled at the lead, impatient to chase the squirrels and explore delicious smells.

Secretly, Francis hoped they'd run into someone he knew, maybe someone from his school who would report seeing him with a pretty girl wearing blue-and-pink leggings and a hip-length black sweater, a girl with *London* tattooed on her left shoulder.

He turned toward her and gave her a kiss on the lips. She laughed. "What was that for?"

"Putting up with Mom's prying questions."

"I like her. I didn't think she was prying, just curious. She's the opposite of my mom. Not tired and sad. I like that she's not afraid to sing her heart out, even if she's tone-deaf."

"And I like you! I like how you always say what you think. I like how you don't judge me."

"Oh, Francis. The secret is that I don't care about what other people think of me. Your mom's the same way." She paused and took a deep breath. "You should try it sometime."

He didn't know what to say to that, so he remained silent. Still, he wished she'd returned his compliment with one of her own, instead of reproaching him.

"Anyway…" Sawyer poked him playfully. "On to something else. I can't wait to meet your dad. Where is he, anyway?" She looked up at him and paused briefly. "You have a dad, right?"

"Yeah, but he's away a lot. No mystery. He's a pilot."

"Nice. So you get free flights and stuff?"

"In principle, but we don't travel too much. My brothers are a handful, even at home on the ground. It's not as exciting as it sounds." Francis sighed. "I wish he were home more, though." He tugged on Ralph's lead. "Slow down, boy. We're almost there."

"Be happy you've got a dad," Sawyer retorted, her face twisted in a sour smile. "Not having one is worse."

He'd noticed that the word *dad* was some kind of trigger for her. He got that she missed her father, but he didn't want to get into it with her right now. He wasn't in the mood for a big discussion about what a jerk her dad had turned out to be. Instead, he nodded in agreement. "Yeah, I know. I am."

That satisfied her and the moment passed. Francis breathed a sigh of relief, and they continued in silence to the park. By the time they got there, Ralph's excitement had reached a fever pitch. "Okay, boy. You're free now." Francis unclipped his leash and Ralph let out a joyous yip before he galloped over the long grass toward the trees.

"Look," Sawyer said, laughing. "I swear that dog is smiling."

"He loves this place almost as much as I do," Francis explained. "And he'll spend the next hour sniffing around to see if any of his friends were here today. See?"

Ralph trotted over to a gnarled tree, sniffed, and lifted his leg.

"Nice," observed Sawyer.

"He's marking his territory."

Sawyer kissed him on the lips. "Me too."

They sat down at a picnic table under the dark branches of an old-growth cedar while Ralph tore around them in circles, sneezing with excitement, his breath hanging in the cool evening air. Francis found a sturdy stick and threw it as far as he could, hampered by the fact that he had one arm, his pitching arm, around Sawyer.

"He could do this for hours," he said, pulling her closer.

"So could I." Sawyer leaned against him and wrapped her leg around his.

Before Sawyer, Francis had never even held hands with a girl. He'd held hands with his mom when he was a kid, maybe his dad, and, of course, Nate and Devon, but this didn't feel anything like that. "Well…," he started "so…"

Sawyer knew what he was talking about, even before he said it. "It wasn't so bad, was it? I expected a lot worse. I thought you didn't want me to meet your family because they were weird or awful or something."

How could he tell her the truth—that he'd been afraid that his mom might not like her—or worse yet, let on that she didn't approve of him having a girlfriend at all?

Politeness had won out. He was sure Sawyer had no idea of his mom's true feelings. He did, though. He knew exactly what she'd say. "*Fifteen is too young to get serious about one person.*"

She'd already made it clear that she wasn't pleased with the amount of time he'd been spending away from home. Since that night when Sawyer so boldly asked him to dance, they'd spent almost every day together after school, usually at Sawyer's apartment on her tattered living room couch, or better yet, on her narrow bed.

As if reading his mind, Sawyer spoke up. "I know why you like being at my place better." Her face clouded over. "I hope you like me for more than just 'afternoon delight.'"

He felt the color rise to his cheeks. "Of course I do—it's not just that. I like that we have your apartment to ourselves, because it means we can be alone together."

She considered his response and smiled. "Good. And don't worry about your mom; she will get to like me."

"Maybe." He sounded doubtful. "I hope so."

"She will. Once she gets over the fact that I'm poor and have a single mom and wear weird clothes." A note of bitterness crept into her voice. "*Oh, we love London.*" She did a perfect job of mimicking his mom's tone of voice and body language.

Francis felt ashamed and shocked that she'd read the situation so well. "You're taking it the wrong way. She's weird, but she's not mean."

"I know. I'm sorry."

Ralph flopped down at their feet, panting. Sawyer caressed his floppy ears. "Like velvet." She yawned, pulling out her phone. "God, it's only six. It feels like eleven." She stood up. "Time to *frappe la rue*. I've got a ton of homework, and I promised my mom I'd do dinner." She turned to him with a frown. "I bet you've never cooked a meal in your life."

"That's because my mom loves to cook." He looked bewildered. "I guess. I never really thought about it."

"Not my mom. She's wiped out after an eight-hour shift at the library."

"You never told me your mom is a librarian."

"That's because she's not. She's a clerk. But she loves books, so that's okay."

"If you're both tired, order in. Chinese or pizza or Indian. That's what we do, like three nights a week minimum."

"Not everyone is a millionaire, Francis." Sawyer moved slightly away. "Not everyone can do exactly as they please, just because they feel like it."

Oh no, here we go again, Francis thought. *I can't say the right thing no matter what.* Sighing, he attempted to defend himself. "I didn't mean—"

She cut him off. "Oh, yes you did. You've got everything, but you don't appreciate anything. You're kind of spoiled, you know. Actually, really spoiled. Must be nice, being in the one percent and all."

Her sudden flash of temper caught him off guard. "Hey! I'm not complaining about my life. And for your information, I'm at Hudson on a scholarship. We've got money, but not as much as you seem to think." Ralph whined and pushed his damp nose against Francis's leg. "And, you're upsetting my dog." He gave Ralph a halfhearted pat on the head.

"One more thing you forgot to mention: you're a brainiac too—a scholarship student, no less." She dropped her chin into her hand. "Forget it. I don't know what's wrong with me. Actually, that's not true. It's just that you don't know how lucky you are. At least compared to me." Her voice hardened. "Just forget I said anything."

"I don't even know what we're arguing about, so it will be easy to forget."

She thrust her chin forward and glared at him. "We're arguing because you don't tell me anything!" Anticipating his objection, she held up her hand like an angry crossing guard. "I didn't know, for example, that you have two adopted brothers who are super-cute or that you live in an almost-mansion or that you go to Europe, instead of the beach or a movie for vacations, or that you're on scholarship at your hoity-toity school for boys! I don't appreciate my boyfriend keeping secrets. I'm calling you on it."

"Fine. But my family is off-limits. Don't imitate my mom." He struggled to keep his voice even.

"Oh, now you're trying to tell me what I can and can't do? Grow up! At least I say what I think."

"So do I," he protested.

"Seriously?" Francis could see she was furious. "I know you think my mom and I are cute and underprivileged. I know you think our apartment is quaint and bohemian, but you'd hate to have a bar across the street from your house, wouldn't you?" She stood up and turned her back to him. "Don't even bother to answer that."

Francis leapt up, his patience gone. "Bullshit. I never said that, none of it."

"My point. You think it, but you don't even have the guts to say it."

"Okay. Fine. True that. Happy now? News flash: I'm with you because I want to be with you, not because of where you live or any of that crap. Yes, we're different, but how is that my fault?" He grabbed Ralph by the collar. "I'm outta here! Come on, Ralph."

"Go, if you want to." Sawyer stood perfectly still, watching him, daring him to leave.

"Fine. Come on, boy." He stormed off, sneaking a parting look her way as he left the park. Sawyer was nowhere in sight. She'd left. He'd blown it. He should have stuck around and finished the fight. "Shit! Ralph, I'm such an idiot."

Ralph licked his hand as if to say, "*No, you're not.*" At least, that's how Francis chose to read it. And how much of an idiot was he, really? It was Sawyer who was hung up on money and house size and crap like that, not him. He hadn't done anything to deserve her anger except the one thing he'd dreaded doing— taking her to his turf to meet his family. What a mistake.

When he got home, his mood hadn't improved. The

shrieks of the twins splashing and squealing meant bath time. Softly, he crept up the stairs, hoping not to attract any attention, but his mom heard him. "Is that you, Francis?" she called. "I could use some help in here."

"Sure." Reluctantly, he entered the twins' bathroom. Despite his bad mood, the sight of his brothers splashing in the bath brought a slight smile to his face. "God, there's water everywhere. Why can't you guys keep it in the tub?"

His mom, perched on a chair just out of reach of the splash zone, sighed. "The million-dollar question. Can you grab some old towels to soak up some of it?"

"I don't see the point until they're out." Francis plunked himself down on the other chair. "Don't get me wet, guys," he warned.

"Like this?" Nate splashed him. Devon followed suit.

"You're just putting ideas into their heads," his mom said, laughing. When he didn't respond, she looked at him more carefully. "How was your walk?"

"I don't want to talk about it."

She tossed a towel at him. "Okay." She paused. "Let's get these guys out and ready for bed."

While they dried the boys, Francis and his mom chatted. At least, his mom did. Francis listened. "Sawyer is an interesting girl—a little out there, but nice—and I can see she has a brain in her head. I know you've been spending a lot of time with her, and I feel better about it now that I've met her." Without skipping a beat, she added, "I assume you've been to her house. Have you met her parents?"

The last thing Francis wanted to do was discuss his girl-friend after they'd had a big fight. For all he knew, Sawyer had already dumped him. But he knew his mom wouldn't stop digging until he offered her a few tidbits.

"Yes, I've been to her house, and no, I haven't met her parents. Not yet. Her mom works at the main library downtown, and Sawyer never talks about her dad. They're divorced. I think he had a drinking problem, but for all I know, he's dead."

Her brow creased. "So there are no adults when you go there?"

"Don't worry, Mom. Nothing's going to happen. Nate, keep still so I can get your pajamas on." His little brother wiggled out of his grasp, giggling.

"Where do they live?"

"Over on Main!" he yelled, chasing Nate out of the bathroom and down the hall.

His mom followed, carrying Devon like a football beneath her arm. "That's a long way." She used a pick to detangle Devon's hair. "Don't move your head," she told him. "It only hurts if you pull away." She turned her attention back to Francis. "Do they live in a house?"

"Yes." White lie. They did technically live in a house, maybe not the whole house, but a house. "It's this cool, old blue-and-white Victorian place."

"Does she have any brothers or sisters?"

"Nope. It's only her." He did his best to wrestle Nate into his pajamas, but his brother had other ideas. "Is the inquisition over yet?"

"Yes, Francis, it's over. Although in my opinion, fifteen is too young to get serious about one person."

He rolled his eyes, taking care that she didn't see him. "Okay, I get it. Is that all?"

"For now. Can you read the boys a story?"

"No, I can't. I've got homework and it's getting late."

"No worries. You concentrate on your homework and I'll wrangle them into bed. Your dinner is in the oven. By the way, Dad called. He says good night. Maybe you could send him a quick text."

"Yeah, I will." That's how he communicated with his dad—text messages, less often a real phone call. No matter. They didn't have much to say to each other.

It took twenty more minutes, but at last Francis managed to get Nate into his pajamas and escape the rest of the chaos of bedtime. He rescued his dinner from the oven and took it up to his room to study, but he found it impossible to concentrate. He sent a short text to his dad, then a longer one to Sawyer:

> *Sorry for being a jerk. I shouldn't have taken off like that. And yes, U R right. I guess I can be a bit judgmental. I don't mean to be secretive, though... I hope U R feeling better. Please forgive?* 😧

She replied immediately.

Of course I forgive you. I can be a jerk too, and there are things you don't know about me either. I'm just tired. Come over tomorrow? 😐

Relieved, Francis typed a message back.

C U after school. 😌

Feeling better, he stretched out on his bed and let his mind drift back to the first time he'd gone to Sawyer's house without her at his side to direct him. He'd taken a bus, something he didn't do often. He'd gotten totally lost. On her side of town, the trees weren't quite as leafy and the lots were long and narrow, like parking spaces. You could hear the neighbors talking and laughing or arguing through the leaded glass windows, and fresh laundry fluttered in the wind on sunny days. When he'd finally arrived, she accused him of being late.

Unthinking, he'd said, "I didn't even know this area existed before you showed it to me. And I wasn't really paying much attention that first time." He smiled cheekily. "You distract me. Anyway, I got on the wrong bus. I mean, I grew up here, but I had no idea Vancouver had such a funky part of town."

He remembered how Sawyer had narrowed her eyes. "Funky?" she scoffed. "I'm going to take that as a compliment rather than assume you meant it literally."

Sawyer and her mom lived in a turn-of-the-century wooden house on Main Street. Like the other homes on the block, theirs had been converted to apartments when the price of real estate in Vancouver had shot up, making it difficult for most people to buy a home. They lived on the top floor, overlooking the busy thoroughfare below. The single-pane windows failed to shut out the cacophony of the busy street—especially late at night when the bars closed and throngs of revelers poured out onto the crowded street.

When Francis first saw her apartment, he wondered how two people managed to live together in such a cramped space and not kill each other. Of course, he didn't say that. Instead, he enthused, "Wow. This is different. Really cool!"

Sawyer saw through his remarks. "We're happy here, Francis. It might not look like much to you, but I love it." She led him to her bedroom window. "At night I crawl out onto the roof. I watch the action. See over there?" She pointed. "That bar gets really sick bands. On a Saturday night, when the weather is good, I leave my window open and fall asleep listening to funk, rock, and indie bands. The noise would drive most people crazy, but not me. Sometimes, after the first set, people come out to smoke, catch sight of me on the roof, and wave. Other times, they have too much to drink and start a fight. Eventually, someone calls the cops. It's like reality TV but better. I love it here," she repeated. "Not everyone lives on the West Side, Francis."

He rolled his eyes. "Give me a break. That's not what I meant." Although he supposed it was.

• • •

Francis bused to her house the next day. He was still thinking about yesterday's conversation and it worried him. The tension between him and Sawyer wasn't good. Maybe his mom had a point; maybe fifteen *was* too young to be in love. On top of this he felt guilty ditching Kevin—and, to be honest, a little resentful at Kevin's neediness. His dad wasn't doing well. But Francis couldn't find the time to visit—not his proudest moment.

A text from Sawyer interrupted his thoughts: *C U at the bus stop. Have to pick up some things @ store.* Ten blocks later, when he alighted from the bus, she was waiting for him.

"Hiya." She pulled him into a long, wet kiss.

Francis noticed that she wasn't heavily made up, and he thought she looked even prettier without the raccoon eyes. "You're so hot," he said, relieved there were no bad feelings left behind from their walk in the park.

At the little market beside her house, they picked up a fresh baguette and a jar of strawberry jam. It was on the tip of Francis's tongue to confess that he'd only ever eaten baguettes in France, but he stopped himself; she'd been right about one thing yesterday—he was pretty lucky, and his luck was a sensitive subject for her.

They took the jam and bread back to her apartment and ate it at the tiny kitchen table overlooking Main Street. Sawyer melted a dark chunk of chocolate into a pot of steaming-hot milk. "This takes more time than store-bought," she said apologetically, "but it's worth it; you'll see. It's my dad's recipe. He loved to cook, back in the day." Her voice faded. "Not that he was around much. I think of him as a cloud that got wispier and wispier until *poof!*—gone. Kind of like your dad, except *he* shows up now and again."

"Yup." *Let's not go there*, he said to himself. He prayed his enthusiastic nod would convince her, but she stopped stirring the hot chocolate and turned to him, her head cocked to one side. "Do you actually know what I mean?"

"I get the analogy," he offered. He nodded again, harder this time. "It's a good one," he added, hoping he sounded authentic.

"Brilliant." Sawyer smiled. She turned her attention back to the hot chocolate, turning the flame down on the old gas stove. "It's easy to scald the milk and then it's almost impossible to clean the pot."

Francis crept up behind her and wrapped his arms around her soft waist. "Would you like to tell me about your dad?" He kissed the top of her head.

Sawyer kept stirring the chocolate in the pot. "When Dad left, he took his favorite things: his Swiss Army knife, his Blue Bombers jersey, the silver flask my mom bought in a Salvation Army store for his fortieth birthday, and his worn leather jacket. I didn't care too much about the knife, or the jacket, but it pissed me off that he didn't take anything to remind him of us. Of me."

Francis breathed in her hair—rose shampoo. "Like a photo, you mean?"

"Hmm." She shivered, and Francis held her tighter.

"Go on," he encouraged.

"The sad thing is, and I've never told anyone this before, I used to wish him dead. He wasn't exactly what you'd call a good provider, not like your dad. He worked on and off at different jobs, but he always got fired in the end, or he quit. It drove my mom nuts. They fought all the time. That's what I remember— them yelling at each other over the sound of traffic."

"I know what that's like," Francis said sympathetically. "My mom and dad used to fight a lot, but not so much anymore, not since we adopted the twins."

Sawyer licked the spoon. "Yeah, it would be pretty hard to be angry around those two. Anyway, you've heard of Western, right?"

"The university?"

"Yeah. The one in *my* London. Dad got a job there. A job he liked for a change. A line chef. Sometimes days would go by and we wouldn't see each other at all. I'd be in school when he was in bed, and when I'd get home, he'd be gone. Sometimes I'd get up in the morning and there would be a doughnut or a slice of pie on the kitchen counter that he'd left for me. There were notes too, describing what happened that day. *Worked late. Tired. Leftovers in fridge.* Or, *Exam today. Studied hard. Thanks for the pastries,* from me. On rare occasions, he'd say how he was feeling: *Tired out. Crazy night. Manager quit. Fed up with dealing with these flakes.* Or I'd say: *Thinking of quitting soccer. Lost game this afternoon. Why does everyone want to blame the goalie?*"

"That's something," Francis said. "I mean, you were thinking about each other."

"It drove my mom crazy." Sawyer shrugged. "He never left notes for her."

"Did she ever leave notes for him?"

"Not sure. I think she tried to make it work, but she couldn't handle the fighting. Some days she didn't have the energy to get out of bed or to brush her teeth. It was awful. Of course, I was little; I didn't understand depression."

Francis kissed her ear.

She swatted him away. "London was a pretty small city. Mom had been a student at Western too, and that's where she'd met my dad. They were both studying architecture. Western is the kind of school you and your friends will go to one day. It's expensive and preppy, full of rich kids who don't know how lucky they are."

Francis ignored the shot and she kept talking, but as if from a distance.

"Anyway, the really sad thing is, I think my parents were happy, until I came along. That's when my dad started drinking. When I was a little kid, I didn't really notice. It took me twelve years to realize he didn't want me, that it was my fault he left."

Francis strained to hear her last few words. He returned to the table and cut himself another thick slice of bread. "Don't be so hard on yourself," he said, trying to comfort her. "That's behind you now. London is in your past. This is your home now."

"Look." She pulled a photo out of her back pocket, creased with wear. "That," she said, pointing, "is my mom. I'm cuddled up to her. There's my dad, behind us." She laughed. "He's smiling down on us like some old-fashioned patriarch, lord and master of his domain. His eyes are so full of light and laughter, no lines, no shadows. He was a handsome man, don't you think? See how he has both of his hands protectively on my mom's shoulders? See how her head is tilted up toward him, a half smile on her lips. I always wonder if the photographer made them look in love, or if they really were, but deep down I already know the answer."

"Sawyer, I'm sorry." He meant it. "I can be hard on my dad, but he's a good guy. I mean, he's away a lot, but that's his work."

"The weird thing is that my dad had been gone for a week before I even noticed." She swiped at her eyes. "God, how pathetic is that?"

Francis did a mental calculation. "That's seven days or 168 hours, or 10,080 minutes. That's got to be some kind of a record."

"My dad the magician. Disappearing was always the thing he excelled at."

"People fall out of love," Francis said. "You can't blame yourself—it happens."

Sawyer turned off the element under hot chocolate and joined him at the table. "Ah, but I can. I've seen photos of my mom after I was born. She looked totally different: tired, her eyes dark and bruised-looking, her skin gray like cement. She suffered from postpartum depression. Dad had to quit university to look after me as a baby. If I hadn't been born, he wouldn't have been driven to drink."

This whole conversation was miles over Francis's head. He struggled to find the right thing to say, but his phone saved him. "Hold on," he said, keeping the relief out of his voice. "It's my mom texting me. She wants to know where I am."

Sawyer just kept on talking as if she hadn't heard him. He sent his mom a quick reply: *At Sawyer's. I won't be home for dinner.*

Kevin called, his mom texted back. *I hope you're not ignoring him because of that girl.*

He stuck the phone back in his pocket, feeling a twinge of guilt, and turned his attention back to his girlfriend. Her eyes were damp. "It's okay," he said, trying to comfort her, not sure at all what *it* referred to.

"No, it's not," she said. "How can you say that? He just took off." Her voice quavered. "And then we moved here." She started to cry. Francis picked at the crumbs on the table.

"The notes stopped. Everything stopped. Mom kept going to work and I kept going to school. We never talked about him. It was as if he'd died. But I still remember the blackness on the day he left. He was in a mean mood. Mom crying, me hiding in my bedroom, Mom hollering at Dad, and Dad hollering at the world. I put my hands over my ears. 'I hate you,' I told him. 'I wish you were dead.' And then he left and he never came back. My dad walked out on us. He dumped Mom, but he dumped me too. Never contacted us. She crashed. I got what I'd wished for. We left Ontario and moved here to Vancouver because my grandparents live here. And that's the end of the story."

"That sucks, Sawyer." *God, could he sound any lamer?*

She didn't appear to notice; instead, she got up and turned the stove back on. "Keep stirring," she said, wiping her eyes. "There's something I want to show you."

He followed her with his eyes. The apartment was about the size of his living room and kitchen combined: one bathroom, two tiny bedrooms, and a long, narrow room with only the kitchen window to let in light. The table was barely big enough for the two of them to sit at comfortably and it doubled as a desk. She disappeared into her bedroom. He heard her rifling around. He turned off the element, removed the pot from the stove, and dug around the cupboards until he found a mishmash of mugs, cups, and glasses. He took out two, poured the hot chocolate, and sat down. It smelled sweet and rich.

When Sawyer returned, she had a cheap vinyl photo album tucked under her arm. She sat down and pushed the album across the table. "Have a look and tell me what you think."

Francis flipped through the pages of faded photos. The album ended abruptly halfway through. The caption under the last picture read: *Sawyer and her dad. Sawyer, thirteen years old.* The album didn't contain many pictures of her dad. Francis studied them and saw a tall, lean man with dark hair and large hooded eyes a lot like his daughter's, only angrier. Tats decorated both his arms. "He looks like you," Francis ventured. "I mean, there's a family resemblance."

That made her happy. "Do you think so? Thank you! I kept some of his things." She pulled a tattered pouch from her pocket and emptied it on the table. "Go ahead. Take a look at my dad's remains."

Gingerly, Francis rummaged through the contents: a small pile of handwritten notes, a pay stub from the University of Western Ontario, a gold wedding band, a can of shaving foam, a button that read *World's Best Chef*, and a chipped mug that read *Happy Father's Day*.

She took the ring and twirled it on her small thumb. It was too big for her, but she didn't seem to care. She was miles away, in her past. "All of his notes are right here." She picked up the pile in front of her and sifted through them with her fingers. "There aren't a ton, but there are enough."

Francis's cell phone vibrated again. "Hold on a sec." His dad. *Hi Francis. I'm in New York. Did you have a good day at school? Home on Thursday. Mom says you have a girlfriend? Way to go! See you then. XO*

"Your mom again?"

"No. My dad this time." He sent back a quick reply: *School's good. See you Thursday.* "I guess we communicate the same way as you and your dad. Short sentences. Kind of lame, right?"

She sat back in her chair and flicked her hair off her face. Francis thought she was beautiful even if her eyes were red and puffy and her face was splotched from crying. "You do get it. The thing is, Francis, I figured out something: dads aren't that important in the greater scheme of life, but even that's sad."

It is *kind of sad*, he thought. He leaned across the table and stroked her long hair, moving it back off her face. "Do we have time to—?"

"No. Tomorrow. My mom's due home anytime now."

Francis sighed. "Tomorrow's no good. I'm going to Kevin's house. I haven't seen him for ages, and you know…things are pretty rough for him right now."

"That's okay. I'm still not feeling so hot. Say hi to Kevin for me." Sawyer had met Kevin a couple of times. She claimed she liked him. "How is his dad?" She knew Francis didn't like talking about it. She knew it scared him.

"No better," he replied shortly.

"Bring Kevin over one day. It'll probably do him good to get out."

"He's not too social right now; besides, I like being alone with you. Should I cancel tomorrow?" He hated himself for suggesting it, let alone saying it aloud.

"No, Francis. A day apart won't kill us. Besides, your friend needs you, and I should spend some time with *my* friend. He's feeling pretty neglected as well."

Alarm bells went off in Francis's head. "Your friend? *He?* You've never mentioned another friend before."

Sawyer's look was coy. "Haven't I? That's strange because I don't have a ton of friends here, but I do have one. You'll like him. His name is Jack and he's, well…let's say he's got a style all his own. He's got rainbow bangs and he's older. I guess he's my other best friend. But don't worry: I love you both." She winked playfully. "Just in different ways."

Francis spent the bus ride home hating Jack, even though he'd never met him or even heard of him until this afternoon.

Chapter Three

The next day, the temperature dropped. Kevin and Francis headed off to soccer together. Francis didn't mention that he'd totally forgotten they had a practice. Overtop of their soccer gear they wore hoodies, but the thin material did little to keep them warm against the late-fall wind.

"It looks like rain." Francis frowned. "I can smell winter in the air." He'd been struggling to find things to talk about, but his friend didn't take the bait.

Kevin shrugged. He hadn't said a word for two blocks. Francis couldn't tell if his silence was because he couldn't handle his dad's quickly declining health or because he was angry with Francis. He had every right to be. They hadn't seen each other for more than ten days.

He tried a new tactic. "Sawyer says hi." Her name rolled off his tongue easily, and he realized how much he liked saying it.

"How *is* the girlfriend?" Kevin said with a hint of sarcasm.

"She's great. Well, she's got some bug. Always feeling nauseous. But she's great…"

"I got that. She's great." Kevin sneered. He didn't bother to feign interest. This wasn't the Kevin Francis knew, but he decided to cut him some slack. He could tell Kevin didn't really give a damn about anyone at the moment, except his father. After a few more failed attempts at conversation, Francis gave up, but he couldn't help feeling annoyed. Yes, he'd ignored Kevin, and yes, he felt bad about it, but times change. *Let's see what happens when he hooks up with someone*, he thought spitefully.

The boys played on a competitive city team. It was intense, and they had no choice but to put everything aside and focus on the ball during practice. But today, Francis couldn't concentrate. Coach was pissed at him. "Wake up!" he shouted more than once. "No sleeping in the goal!"

Kevin fared better. He played forward with the agility of a dancer, despite his size, while Francis, in goal, had large swaths of time alone in the net to think and to freeze. Finally, practice came to an end, and they packed up their gear for the walk home. Before they left, Coach approached Francis.

"Is everything okay with you?"

"I'm just a bit off today." Francis shrugged. "It happens."

Coach nodded. "I see. And Kevin? How is he doing?"

"Kevin's okay, considering."

"Well, if you need someone to talk to, I'm always ready to listen." He'd been their coach for a long time, and Francis knew he meant it.

"Thanks," he said. "But everything is fine."

Coach narrowed his eyes. "Well, that wasn't reflected in practice today. I'll expect more effort next time." With a stern look, he stomped off.

"What's up with him?" Kevin asked. "His face was bright red."

"Coach is choked with me, but not you. Three goals. Pretty fancy footwork."

"These days, I take out all my frustrations on the field. It works pretty well most of the time." Kevin's voice was devoid of emotion.

Francis felt helpless. He kicked at the damp ground. "I meant to ask, how is your father doing?"

"Yeah. You haven't been around for a while. He's…you'll see when we get to my place. I guess I should prepare you so you don't freak out. He's lost a lot of weight."

"Your dad is a big guy, like you. It's lucky he had some pounds to shed."

"No, you don't get it. I mean a *lot* of weight." Kevin's voice broke and he turned away. "He weighs, like, a hundred and thirty-five pounds. It's not good."

Francis swallowed. Kevin's dad stood over six feet tall.

"He can't eat, not much, anyway." Kevin kicked at a rock. "He's not going to make it. That's what the doctors say. He's not going to be around much longer." He kicked the rock again, harder. It sailed out onto the street, grazing the hood of a parked car. "Fuck. Come on. Let's get out of here."

They made a run for it and didn't stop until they were sure they didn't have an irate car owner on their heels.

"Nice one," Francis said, bending over to catch his breath. "Kevin, I didn't know it was that bad. I mean, should I still come over?"

Kevin didn't answer his friend right away. He just kept on walking.

Kevin and Francis had been best friends since grade four, back when it was all fun and games. No homework, no exams, and no mention of the big C.

When Kevin thought about the big C, he thought of the green Pacific, or the gray, murky Atlantic, or the turquoise-blue Caribbean. Those were "big seas." Cancer had no right to claim bigness. Cancer, Kevin had learned, was no better than a thief who worked slowly, every day taking a little more until there was nothing left.

Already, Kevin could see the skeleton beneath his dad's tissue-thin skin. But if he closed his eyes and blocked out everything, he could still remember his dad's muscular arms, tanned from the hours spent in the garden, his broad shoulders, steadfast smile, his determined and confident walk, his salty scent.

"Kevin, should I come over?"

Kevin blinked. "Sorry, man. Yeah. You should come. My dad wants to see you, but like I said, he doesn't look good. It's better if you try to keep the shock off your face."

"I'm sorry." Francis gripped his friend's shoulder. "Don't worry about me. I'll be cool."

"You know what my dad said to me last week?" Kevin sucked in a mouthful of air. "When he was trying to comfort me, instead of me comforting him, he said, 'Do not despair. Remember what Queen Gertrude in Hamlet said to her son? *Thou know'st 'tis common; all that lives must die. Passing through nature to eternity.'*"

Francis smiled because that's how Mr. Croyden talked, despite everything. He could imagine the exchanges: *Kevin, would you be so kind as to fetch me my painkillers? Kevin, I seem to need a little help sitting up. Do you think you could oblige me?* "Yeah, that sounds like your dad."

Kevin snorted. "Anybody else would be screaming in agony. Anybody else would demand more and more drugs, but not him. I can't imagine a world without him in it. I try to, and it makes me throw up. 'Be brave,' he says. 'Carry on.' I'm trying." His voice broke. "But it's frigging hard."

"I'm sorry."

"Besides," Kevin continued, "my mom's made ribs for dinner. She'd be upset if you didn't show. Just be prepared. Dad will be happy to see you. He's always liked you."

Francis pulled his hoodie up over his head. "I've always liked him too. I think the world of him."

There was no need to remind Kevin how his dad had stood in for Francis's father when they were little kids. How Mr. Croyden coached him in soccer, taught him to skimboard, showed him how to get a decent score on the pitch and putt, or how to get on and off the chairlift without doing a face-plant. "Before the twins came along, I practically lived at your place."

Francis had been a lonely kid. Kevin's family had included him in everything, made him feel like a part of their family.

"Yeah. The thing is, Francis, it's all ending. I don't want to talk about it. The thing is, what can you or anyone say to make it better?"

They continued in silence until they arrived at the Croyden house. Francis did his best to mentally prepare himself, but the moment they stepped inside the front door, he knew that everything had changed. The deathly silence and the cloying smell of sickness assaulted him, and he had to force himself to not turn and run. Instead, he sank down on the bench and put his head between his hands.

"You okay?" Kevin sat down beside him. "Come on. You said you could handle it."

"I'm good. I just need a second."

In that moment, he understood two things: It *was* all ending, and Sawyer was wrong. In the greater scheme of things, dads mattered a whole lot.

"Take off your shoes," Kevin whispered. "My dad sleeps most of the time and we don't like to wake him."

Pull yourself together, Francis ordered himself. *It's worse for Kevin.*

With a deep breath, he stood, forcing his voice to be strong. "Sorry, man. It just hit me."

They padded down the hall in search of Kevin's mom. They found her in her study, standing by the window, her arms wrapped protectively around her body. She was staring out the window at the tall trees that pushed up against the house like sentries. Francis saw her before she saw him. *My god, she's lost a lot of weight.* It shocked him.

"Mom, Francis is here," Kevin said.

Mrs. Croyden turned around slowly, her face wet with tears, but she seemed unaware that she was crying. "Hello. Francis, we've missed you around here." Suddenly her arms were wrapped around him. The tears he'd been choking back flowed freely.

"Oh, Francis. I'm sorry. I know you love him. I know it's impossible. Thank you for coming." She released her hold and held him at arm's length. Her eyes were tired and bloodshot, her skin gray.

Kevin's mom had been a beautiful woman. Francis used to have a crush on her when he was younger. She'd aged a hundred years.

Still she managed a genuine smile. "I'm so happy to see you. Kevin, why don't you take Francis in to see your dad before dinner? He's been waiting. Don't stay very long, though," she added. "He's tired today."

"Worse?"

"A little, honey, but he's excited to see Francis."

"He's in the den," Kevin explained to Francis. "We moved him in there when he couldn't make it upstairs anymore." Francis followed his friend across the hall and waited while he tapped on the door. "Dad? Francis is here to see you. Can we come in?"

"Please do!" Mr. Croyden's voice was weaker than Francis remembered. But the enthusiasm was still audible.

Kevin pushed open the door and entered quietly. Francis paused before following him. Mr. Croyden sounded frail. He hadn't expected that, not from a man known for his hearty voice.

Francis looked around the large, once-familiar den with a sinking heart; he hated this room the way it was now. At least the books remained. Still, he missed the thick Persian carpets and despised the functional hospital bed. The air smelled stale and sharp, like strong cheese and mouthwash. Beside the bed was an IV stand. A solid, no-nonsense nurse greeted the boys with a bright smile. "Come in! Come in." She turned to her patient and said, "We've got visitors."

The frail form under the covers shifted. "I may be dying of cancer, but I can still see. I've asked you to refrain from using the plural when referring to me. All of my senses remain intact, for the moment."

The nurse pursed her lips. "Of course," she snapped. Francis smiled to himself. Kevin's dad hadn't changed all that much.

Kevin rushed to his father's side. "I scored three goals in practice."

"That's my boy. Outstanding, son. Give me a big hug."

Francis positioned himself on the other side of the bed. He wanted to be as far away as possible from the nurse and the tools of her trade. He waited for Kevin to disentangle himself from his dad's embrace before he spoke. "Hi, Mr. Croyden. It's so good to see you."

"Francis!" Mr. Croyden's voice was strained, but he smiled, and the smile reached his sunken eyes. "There you are!"

Francis stuck out his hand. Mr. Croyden laughed weakly. "Let's not stand on formalities. I think we've known each other long enough to merit a hug. I'm so pleased you've come."

Mr. Croyden's body felt like it might break in Francis's arms, but the man still knew how to deliver a strong bear hug. "Now, if you'll move a few feet to your right, I can have a proper look at you."

Francis complied. He thought he'd been ready to see Kevin's dad, but nothing could have prepared him for the skeletal figure beaming up at him from the hospital bed. Only his bright, kind eyes hadn't changed.

Mr. Croyden must have seen his distress because he said, "Stop chomping on your top lip. You've nothing to be afraid of. You look the picture of health." He coughed, regained his breath, and continued. "I hope your game went as well as Kevin's."

"It was a practice, and no," Francis mumbled, unable to get over his disbelief at seeing him so shrunken.

"I can see you're a bit tongue-tied." Mr. Croyden pushed himself up into a semi-seated position, using pillows for support. The nurse stepped in to help, but he waved her away. "Damn it," he winced. "I'm fine to sit up on my own."

Francis looked away, but not before he saw the fine blue veins that bulged just beneath the paper-thin skin on Mr. Croyden's hands.

"Kevin, if you don't mind, I want a private word with your friend. Could you give us a few minutes alone?"

"Sure, Dad. Can I get you anything?"

"You've brought me Francis. Thank you." After a spasm of coughing, his face relaxed.

Don't leave me, Francis wanted to shout as Kevin disappeared out the door.

"I know this is horribly awkward, Francis, and I'm sorry. However, time is of the essence and I'm glad for the chance to say good-bye privately." He gestured for Francis to sit down on the bed. "And I've a favor to ask of you."

"Not good-bye." A lump rose in his throat. "Not good-bye," he repeated.

Kevin's dad reached out and patted his arm. His hand shook with the effort. "It hurts to move," he explained, "but that's got nothing to do with you. This is my journey. Francis, I know how hard this is for you. We've been good friends, you and I, over the years. I've watched you grow into a fine young man." He paused, his breathing labored. "Forgive me. Even talking has become something of a challenge." His body shook with another spasm of coughing.

Francis waited until he'd finished. "I don't know what to say, Mr. C…I mean, you are a second father to me…I don't know how to say good-bye." He sniffled and tried to hide his emotion with a cough.

"Of course you don't. Thank you for your honesty. And you are a second son to me. Now listen to me." His forehead creased with the effort to speak. "When I go, which will be soon, it's going to be exceedingly difficult for Kevin. I don't have to tell you how close we are. The favor I am asking of you is simple: Be there for him. Talk to him, talk about me. It will help him. Remind him of all we've done together. Keep the memory of me alive, because he's going to be angry with me for leaving. It will be easier to go if I know he has a real friend."

He paused. "And most importantly, I know I can count on you both to grow up to be the right kind of men."

His head sank to the pillow. His eyes closed and he sighed heavily. His breath became impossibly loud, drowning out the sound of all the medical technology humming in the background.

Francis took his hand and squeezed gently. "I will. I promise, but…it's just…you can't give up."

"No," Mr. Croyden whispered. "There's a difference between giving up and accepting something. I know I can't win this one, but I'm not afraid. Make sure Kevin knows that, and remind him of how much I loved him. Being his dad was my greatest gift and my greatest accomplishment."

"I will. I'll tell him. I promise."

"Live well, Francis. Do that for me." He opened his eyes. "Go ahead. Say it. I need to hear it."

"Good-bye, Mr. C." His voice caught in his throat. "I love you."

"I love you too, Francis." Mr. C seemed to be shrinking before his eyes, but he managed another smile. "*Bon voyage* is how I prefer to put it."

"Bon voyage," Francis whispered. He sat very still, holding Mr. Croyden's hand until the nurse tapped him on the shoulder.

"He's asleep," she said. "He won't wake up for a few hours. It's time for you to go."

"Bon voyage," he breathed.

Francis left the room with a heavy heart and found Kevin slouched at the kitchen table. A steaming plate of roast potatoes sat untouched in front of him.

Beside Kevin, his mom moved her food slowly around her plate. When Francis walked in, she looked up. "We were just waiting for you. Sit anywhere. It's all very casual at the moment, I'm afraid. Help yourself."

Francis pulled out the nearest chair and sat down. "No apologies."

He helped himself to the ribs and potatoes, not because he was hungry, but because he wanted to make Mrs. Croyden feel better. It worked.

"What a pleasure to feed someone who actually has an appetite!" she exclaimed. "Kevin and I do our best to eat, but it's difficult, what with…"

Kevin finished her thought. "With watching Dad struggle to swallow milky oatmeal or mashed veggies without throwing up." He threw his fork down.

"You'll have to excuse us," his mother apologized. "We don't mean to be rude."

Francis pushed the meat and potatoes around his plate; the food in his mouth tasted like sawdust. Kevin's mom didn't notice, or if she did, she didn't say anything.

"What did my dad say?"

"Another time." Francis excused himself. "I'm glad I came, but I have to go. I'm sorry, but I have to go now."

They seemed as relieved to see him leave as he was to

escape. Kevin didn't get up, but his mother did. She insisted on walking him out. They tiptoed down the hall. Francis held his breath when they passed the room where Mr. Croyden lay dying. He didn't want that terrible smell to be his last memory.

"Thank you, Francis." Kevin's mother opened the front door. Her eyes filled with tears. "It meant so much to my husband to see you one last time."

Francis ran home, knowing that if he slowed down, if he gave himself a second to think, his heart might break.

Chapter Four

Not much distance lay between the Croyden house and the Sloan house, but Francis had to dig deep just to find the energy to keep running. Kevin was right—how was it possible to imagine a world without his father in it?

When Francis arrived, his mom and his brothers were in the kitchen. Nate and Devon squealed with delight at the sight of their older brother.

"Leave me alone," he snapped.

His flat voice stopped them in their tracks.

"Oh, honey." His mom hated to see any of her kids unhappy. "Do you want to talk about it?"

"No." But somehow the details of his visit with Kevin's dad poured out of him.

She listened without interrupting, except to gently shush the twins, and suddenly he'd told her everything. When he'd finished, she sat very still, giving him the chance to collect himself.

"Poor Kevin," she said. "Poor you. It is gut-wrenching for the whole family. Austin is a wonderful man. Is there anything we can do for them—send over some food or anything?"

Restless, Francis got up and leaned against the fridge, his eyes downcast, trying to make sense of it all. "That's the whole problem, Mom. There's nothing to do. He's going to disappear." Despite his effort, a tear leaked out of the corner of his eye. He swiped at it savagely. Crying wouldn't change anything.

Alarmed, Nate ran into his mother's arms. "What's wrong with Francis?"

Devon burst into tears. "Don't cry, Francis." He reached up and wrapped his arms around his big brother's thigh. "Mommy, make him stop crying."

"Your brother is sad," his mother explained. "You cry when you are sad. We all do." She pulled Nate onto her lap and squeezed him. "Hugs help people to feel better."

As usual, his mom was right; Francis did feel slightly better after she got up and hugged him too—until Nate started to climb up his leg. Francis shook him off. "Make tracks, little guy. Go and play with Ralph. Throw his ball for him. He'd love that."

"We don't want to," whined Devon.

"Go and play with the dog in the garden for a little while, and I'll make you a delicious fruit bowl with ice cream," their mom promised.

After some consideration, the twins tore out the back door, Ralph on their heels.

"Seriously, Mom. Bribery? You must be really worried about me." Francis sighed. "I'm okay, though."

"I'll call Kevin's mom in the morning to see what we can do to help. Maybe I'll organize some meals. It's the least I can do. Just think of all the times Austin treated you boys to restaurants after soccer. I could always count on him to take you under his wing when your dad was away on a long trip. It's a terrible tragedy. Austin's been a wonderful dad and a big part of our community. He made things happen." She rubbed her temples as if she had a headache. "That's what I'll do."

Later that evening, Francis thought about what his mother had said. She was right. Until the cancer, things didn't happen to Mr. Croyden unless he wanted them to; he made things happen, he was always in control. *That must be part of the secret of being a good man.*

When his dad called, Francis realized how much he missed him. He wished he could say so, but that would be weird. "Hey," he said instead. "When are you coming home?"

"A few days. Are you all right?" His dad sounded distracted as usual.

"Not really, Dad. I saw Mr. Croyden today. He's losing his battle with cancer. He's days from passing." He hated himself for sugarcoating it. *Passing? Stupid word. He's not passing anything. He's dying.* Francis cleared his throat. "He's going to die soon. I'm worried about Kevin."

"I'm so sorry that I can't be there with you, but I'm glad you told me."

"You sound tired, Dad."

"Long day," he replied. He tried to stifle a yawn. "I wish I could be home, but I can't. Sometimes there's nothing worse than being three time zones away, but I'll be back in a few days. I'll call you in the morning before you go to school. Say, eight-hundred hours?"

After that, there didn't seem a whole lot more to say, so Francis passed the phone to his mom. She reassured his father that Francis would be fine. She added to the details Francis had given and repeated what a terrible tragedy this was for everyone. Before she hung up, she reminded him about his promise to call.

"I don't see why it's up to you to make that happen," Francis scolded.

"You know how hard it is for your dad not to be here," she replied. "Sometimes harder for him than for you guys."

At breakfast the next morning, Francis put his phone beside his bowl of cereal. "Dad's supposed to call," he told the twins, checking his watch. "In approximately twelve minutes."

"Yay," they chorused.

"I get to talk to him first," shouted Nate.

"I get to talk to him second," chimed in Devon.

Francis rolled his eyes. "We'll all get a turn."

By ten past eight, the phone hadn't rung. By 8:25, Francis knew it wouldn't, but he checked again at 8:45—just in case he'd accidently put it on silent mode. Nothing.

"Why don't you call him?" his mom suggested.

The phone went right to voice mail.

"He must have slept in," his mom offered weakly. "He does

his best." She straightened Francis's school tie and gave him a light peck on the cheek. "Off you go, or you'll be late for school, and don't forget your lunch. I've put a special treat in today."

"I'm not five, Mom, but thanks."

"Francis, don't be too hard on your father. I know he meant to call. He was terribly upset to hear about Austin."

"Whatever." This wasn't the first time he'd been let down by a phone call that never happened. "Guess what…I don't care. Right now, I'm more worried about Kevin than I am about myself." He stormed out of the room, calling over his shoulder, "And by the way, I'm going to Sawyer's after school."

"Will her mother be home?"

"Mom, we've already talked about this. Besides, I'm fifteen. I don't need a babysitter anymore."

For the last time, he checked his phone. Nothing from his dad, but there was a text from Sawyer: *I saw a huge bumblebee.*

They always made him laugh, her random texts. *My house 2nite?*

C U after school, he replied, surprised at how much he wanted to be with her.

• • •

Hudson Preparatory School was an imposing gray stone building with two towering turrets that overlooked the swimming pool and the park beyond. Francis had worked hard to pass the scholarship exams, and every day he was grateful to be a member of the student body. He loved the wood-paneled classrooms, the quiet study halls, and the soaring stained-glass windows that glowed over the perfectly groomed playing fields. But his favorite place was the library, with its comfy chairs, large sofas, and floor-to-ceiling shelves that groaned from the weight of thousands of books.

It was the perfect spot to study or think or escape the chaos of three hundred boys. Because his first class was a spare, he went there right after assembly, relieved to see that no other students occupied his usual spot, a worn leather sofa behind the bookshelves in the dimly lit history section.

Mr. Haywood Smith, or HS as the boys called him, seemed as old and knowledgeable as the books he safeguarded. When Francis walked in, he gave him a friendly nod. "Good morning, Mr. Sloan. I hope that's not a phone in your hand?"

Francis stuffed his phone into his blazer pocket. "Of course not, Hay. By the way, I've got a spare, so I thought I'd spend some time in my favorite chair."

The aged academic's eyebrows creased. "Hay, my boy, is for horses, and I have a name."

"Yes, sir. Sorry, sir. Good morning, Mr. Haywood Smith," he intoned in his best private school voice.

"Politeness is the sine qua non of civilization."

"Yes, Mr. Haywood Smith. I agree entirely with Mr. Heinlein."

"Well done." HS, who spent his days buried in the stacks, shuffled off.

Relieved to be alone, Francis settled on the couch, leaned back, and closed his eyes, listening to the muted sounds around him: pages turning, a swallow scolding outside the window, the whispered conversations of other boys, and the occasional throat-clearing from Haywood Smith. Although he let his thoughts roam freely, they kept returning to Kevin's dad, to his emaciated frame and hollow eyes, to his shaking hands and feeble voice. To his final request.

What had he meant when he said, "I know I can count on the two of you to grow up to be the right kind of men"? *What*, Francis wondered, *is the right kind of man? A man like his father—stoic, dependable, decisive, trustworthy, strong?* Francis knew his dad was a good dad because he provided stability. *A man like Mr. Croyden—loving, warm, wise, funny, educated, athletic?* Mr. Croyden was a good dad because he gave time.

What about the disappeared men—the ones you couldn't see? Sawyer's dad didn't even rate, and yet she loved him, sort of. The twins must have had a dad somewhere in Africa, but no mention had ever been made of him.

Maybe, for most guys, it was difficult to be a good man and a father at the same time.

In the end, he didn't have an answer. *But I'm never having kids*, Francis concluded. *It's too hard.*

Being a scholarship student was difficult. Unlike the boys whose parents paid tuition, Francis had to excel in all of his courses. If he didn't, he'd lose his place. He couldn't afford another minute pondering philosophical questions. His classes were not easy, and exams were just around the corner. For the rest of the day, he concentrated on his studies and put everything else, including his date with Sawyer, out of his mind.

But when the final bell rang, Francis tore out of school and made a beeline for the bus stop. The ride to her apartment took forever, but at last he arrived, out of breath from racing up the stairs. "I missed you all day," he panted when she opened the door.

She looked so pretty, kissable, even though she hadn't combed her hair and she was kind of pale.

She grabbed his arm and pulled him into the room and onto the couch, planting a wet kiss right on his lips. "I like you," she bubbled. "I seriously like you. I've never actually had a boyfriend I liked before."

A warning bell went off in Francis's head. "I've never had a girlfriend at all," he admitted. "But if I had, I hope I would have liked her."

"It doesn't always work that way," she said wistfully. "But now you have me." She leaned back against the cushion and closed her eyes. "I wish this flu would go away. I'm so tired all the time."

"I thought you were feeling better. Maybe you need a nap." He ran his hand over her soft thigh, only half-teasing.

She jerked her leg away. "You'd better not mess with me, Francis. Don't disappear on me."

Francis made a face. "Not every guy is an asshole. You don't have to worry about me."

She sighed and muttered something under her breath that he didn't catch.

"Come here," he said. "Let's not argue. Not today."

She leaned into him, so close that when he closed his eyes, he could feel the length of her body.

"I love you," she whispered, and her soft breath tickled his ear.

Francis nodded, unable to speak, and gathered her into his arms. Things got a little heated after that. Seriously hot.

• • •

A half hour later, Francis and Sawyer lay on the tattered couch, toe-to-toe, knee-to-knee, nose-to-nose. They remained like that until Francis's arm began to go numb. Reluctantly, he sat up, pulling Sawyer beside him. He ran his fingers through her hair. It was mussed up, but he didn't mind. She looked beautiful. He told her so, and she smiled.

"You're sweet. But on a more serious note," she said, gazing, up at him, "I was thinking that…there's something I need to talk to you about."

Francis groaned inwardly, but he gave her an encouraging nod. "Your shirt is undone," he pointed out, not really listening to her at all.

"Francis, I'm trying to have a conversation with you!"

"And I can't focus if you don't cover yourself up!"

She did up the buttons on her shirt. "Better?"

He grinned. "Shoot."

"Okay, as I was trying to say—" Sawyer stopped midsentence. "Oh god."

They both heard it at the same time. The unmistakable rasp of a key turning in the front door lock.

"Shit! Mom's home." Sawyer leapt off the couch. "Go sit at the table," she whispered urgently, plumping up the couch cushions. "Oh god. She'll kill us if she catches us. Cover for me. I'll be back in a sec."

She sprinted into the bathroom while Francis scrambled to the table, knocking over a lamp in the process. "Shit," he cursed, quickly righting it.

From behind him a voice boomed. "Who on earth are you?"

Francis spun around and found himself face-to-face with an older and much fiercer version of Sawyer. "Who am I?" he stammered.

Sawyer's mom crossed her arms. She was petite, dressed for work in a blue blazer and gray skirt. Her hair, the same color and texture as Sawyer's, was closely cropped. Businesslike was how he would later describe her to Kevin—no-nonsense, the kind of person who would shush you in the library, even though she was only a clerk. The kind of person you'd listen to if you had even half a brain.

"Are you an idiot?" She wasn't smiling.

"No. I'm Francis." He realized he really sounded like an idiot.

"Oh. Well, hello, Francis. Who are you, and what are you doing in my apartment? What did you do with that lamp? Where's my daughter?" It was like being under cross-examination in a criminal court.

"I'm your daughter's...BF. I'm Francis." He stuck out his hand.

"Ah, *boyfriend* is the word I think you are looking for. No last name? Are you like Drake or Shad?"

"Sloan. Francis Sloan."

"Hello, Francis Sloan, or should I call you the Sloan Ranger?" She cackled at her own joke and her hand closed over his. "I'm Mrs. Martin."

She had a grip like a vice. It reminded him of Mr. Croyden's, and Francis liked her for that, despite his terror.

"What exactly have you two been up to?"

"Uh."

"Don't give him a hard time, Mom," Sawyer yelled from the bathroom. "He's kind of naive and sheltered. You'll scare him for life."

Mrs. Martin's face softened. "Oh, the private-school kid and much-talked-about boyfriend. What's the name of that fancy school again?"

"Stop interrogating my guest," Sawyer shouted, slamming the bathroom door.

Mrs. Martin's face took on a mask of innocence. "I'm doing no such thing. I think it's nice that you've brought a friend home, but I wish you had let me know."

Sawyer appeared in the doorway. She'd brushed her hair and straightened her clothes. There was color in her cheeks. "You're home early, Mom."

Mrs. Martin raised her eyebrows. "I was worried about you when you didn't go to school today, but you look like you're feeling better now."

Sawyer hadn't mentioned skipping school. Why? Weren't they supposed to share those kinds of things? Now was not the time to ask. Now was the time to get out as quickly as possible.

"Much better, thanks." Sawyer sat down at the table and took Francis's hand. He resisted, pulling it away. She turned to her mom with wide, innocent eyes. "Remember I told you I thought I might be in love?"

"I recall something like that, Sawyer."

"Well, Mom, this is the lucky boy."

When she turned back to him, Francis was sure she could smell his fear.

"Not too lucky, I hope." Mrs. Martin didn't blink. Just kept staring.

Francis squirmed. He blushed. His heart sped up, and his hands began to sweat.

Sawyer saved him. "Don't listen to my mom. She's trying to make you uncomfortable. Stop it, Mom. We're twin flames, so you'll have to get used to him being around. Isn't that right, Francis?"

"Huh? I guess." He shot her a pleading look that said, *I don't know what you're talking about and I don't care. Get me out of here. Now.*

Sawyer smiled. "Twin flames."

Mrs. Martin's expression turned from anger to—was he imagining it?—pity. "She's referencing Zeus, Francis. According to Greek mythology, we're all searching for our soul mate—our twin flame—but take it from me, it's not that simple. Here's how I see it. At first you love someone so much they consume

72

you, and then later, unless you are very lucky, you hate them so much that they *do* consume you, but in a bad way."

Francis listened to her, but he didn't understand a word she said. "Oh," he managed.

"Mom, don't be so maudlin," Sawyer scolded. "Lucky for Francis, he was just leaving."

Grateful, Francis jumped up. "Yeah. I was just on my way out." He bolted for the door.

"Wait!" Sawyer's mom ordered.

His heart lurched to a stop. "Yes?"

She grinned at him. "You might need this. It's raining." She plucked his jacket off the back of the couch.

"Thank you," he blurted and turned to go.

"And this." She handed him his backpack.

Sawyer suppressed a giggle. "See you later."

"Bye," Francis managed to choke out. "Nice to meet you, Mrs. Martin."

"I bet it was. Sorry you have to run off." She nodded curtly.

The door slammed shut behind Francis, and he found himself alone in the hall, guilty as hell. His breathing didn't return to normal until the bus pulled away from the curb and turned toward the West Side.

"That," he breathed, "was way too close a call."

The streetlights came on while the bus rolled across the city. Outside, the rain glimmered on the black roads. It was later than Francis thought. His mother would not be pleased with him. His mind wandered. Francis wondered what it was that

Sawyer had seemed so eager to talk to him about before they were interrupted. She could be so serious sometimes.

He hoped it wasn't more about her dad; she clearly had some pretty deep-rooted issues around his abrupt departure. Her tone had verged on threatening when she'd said "Don't disappear on me."

As if. He'd spend every second of every day with her if he could. He decided to look up Zeus as soon as he got home so he would understand what Sawyer and her mother meant with all of that talk about soul mates and flames.

In the meantime, he had a lot to think about. Having a girlfriend was great, but it came, he decided, with a lot of unexpected complications. He sighed so loudly that the woman in the seat in front of him turned around with a worried look. "Are you okay?"

"Yes. Sorry," he mumbled.

For example, he didn't get the chance to ask her about that dude, Jack. That must have been what she wanted to talk about.

Overhead, clouds gathered and the rain grew heavier. Inside the bus, the heat and breath of the passengers clung to the windows, and he couldn't see a thing. Francis shivered, though the air in the bus was warm and sticky.

If only Kevin's dad wasn't sick. If only Kevin wasn't mad at him. If only Sawyer wasn't so unpredictable. She should have told him that she'd skipped school.

If only he didn't have to deal with the unwelcome intrusion of a boy named Jack. If only life could be more simple.

Chapter Five

Francis had two good reasons for a girlfriend break. Number one, he had no desire to run into Sawyer's mother for a while. It hadn't been a stellar first meeting. And number two (and he knew this was selfish), he didn't want to catch whatever strange bug Sawyer had—not with exams looming.

He called her up, somewhat wary about her reaction to his idea. He had expected some attitude, but to his relief, she agreed. To his disappointment, she did so without hesitation. Still, he managed to hide his displeasure, along with his suspicion that Jack probably had something to do with her acquiescence.

"Great." He made his voice light, and quickly changed the subject. "By the way, what did you want to talk to me about the other day, before your mom got home?"

"It can wait," she said, "at least until I see you again."

"Okay. It won't be long. I just have to get some serious studying in."

"Same," replied Sawyer. "My mom's been bugging me to hit the books, and so has Jack."

"And I need to spend some time with Kevin and his dad," Francis acknowledged.

"Okay. Text me when you're around." She hung up, and Francis couldn't help but feel a twinge of insecurity, or was it jealousy?

At least his mom would be relieved to have him around again after school for a while, and he really did need to spend more time with Kevin.

Except Kevin's dad was no longer well enough to have visitors. "Wait until he is a little stronger," Kevin said apologetically, but they both knew that ship had sailed.

Francis and Sawyer didn't see each other all week, or on the weekend. They texted daily and talked on the phone at night, but Sawyer was usually tired and cranky by ten o'clock. He attributed her moodiness to her increasingly poor health and she confirmed this when she confessed she'd had to miss a few days of school. "I was, like, puking and felt really sick."

"Maybe you should see a doctor," he suggested.

"Maybe. That's what Jack says too."

"Well, then it must be true," Francis snapped. *Always Jack.* He knew he was acting like an idiot, but he couldn't help it.

When he didn't hear from Sawyer all the next day, he panicked and sent her a text. *When R U around? I can't wait much longer to C U.*

Her answer came quickly. *I miss U 2. Come over anytime, but Mom's working late tomorrow.*

His stomach did a slow flip. That night, he slept better than he had for a long time. The next day after school, he called his mother and told her not to expect him for dinner. He didn't have to tell her why. As a mom, she used her sixth-sense thing to figure it out.

"Oh," she grumbled. "I thought maybe you two had broken up."

"No such luck, Mom."

The bus ride across town seemed longer than ever. When he arrived, he bolted up the stairs and banged on Sawyer's door. She threw it open and fell into his arms. "You're here!"

For a long time, they stood in the doorway and kissed, and then Sawyer pulled him inside. "How did your exams go?"

"Great." But he didn't want to talk about school.

"I'm glad we don't have midterms like you guys," Sawyer said. "School's hard enough right now without a bunch of tests."

He was surprised. Sawyer was bright, a straight-A student. "What's going on?"

"Remember?" She put her hands on her hips and sighed. "I've been sick." She had every right to be frustrated with him.

"Sorry," he said. "I knew that."

"That's okay. I've got a surprise for you."

She was flushed and excited, but her high color had nothing to do with Francis's arrival and everything to do with someone else's. "Today is the day you get to meet Jack! He'll be here soon, and you're going to love him."

Francis didn't bother to hide his disappointment. "Oh, perfect. It's been a week, almost two, since I saw you. I thought we'd be alone."

She gave him a gentle push, and he sank into the couch. "Sometimes, Francis, I think the only thing you think about is sex."

"I just don't get why this guy has to come over right now." He was whining, but he couldn't help it.

"He wants to meet you. Unlike you, he's friendly. Anyway, don't worry. You'll adore him as much as I do. I promise. And you'll see that he is no threat."

"I never said that he was."

"No. You didn't have to. It's in your expression, your tone of voice, and your body language. Please, Francis, try. It means a lot to me."

He glanced up at her and saw that she really wanted him to cooperate. "Fine," he agreed with a frown, "but I hope he doesn't stay long." It took a lot to even concede this.

Outside, a dog barked. Someone yelled, "Keep that mutt on a leash before it gets run over!"

Francis chuckled. "I've missed being here, and I've missed you," he said.

"Same." She sat down and curled up beside him. When her lips touched his, his temper cooled, and for a long, delicious moment, he forgot to be annoyed.

And then she pulled back. "Sorry. I'm still not feeling great."

She brushed her hair off her face, and he noticed she'd lost her earlier color. "Are you okay?" he asked, suddenly scared.

"It comes and goes." She shook her head. "Mom thinks maybe I have some kind of allergy, or that maybe the food at the corner store isn't exactly fresh. Whatever it is, I'm tired of it."

"Maybe eating dinner at the corner store isn't the best thing," Francis joked, half-meaning it.

"Easy for you to say. You have a personal chef called Mom."

Francis stroked her cheek. "You're right. How much time do we have until this guy shows up?"

"Enough time to talk," she answered, her lip trembling. "We have to talk."

"We can talk after," Francis suggested hopefully.

"No, Francis. It's kind of important."

He sighed and sat back in the couch, prepared to listen. "Okay. I'm all ears."

"Well, last week, my teacher asked me to stay after school…I knew she wasn't too pleased with me; I'd missed some classes and tests, and my marks had dropped."

She closed her eyes. Francis waited patiently, aware of the ticking of the old clock on the wall opposite him.

After a lengthy pause, she continued. "I've always been top of the class. She attributed my poor performance to moving and changing schools. I should have gone along with that, but, stupidly, I told her I'd adjusted just fine. She wanted to know if anything else was bugging me, and I told her the truth—you know, that I'd been sick with this low-grade bug since the start of the school year and that, as result, I was having trouble concentrating. And you know what she said?" She gave him a sad half smile. "Just like the rest of you, she told me I should go and see a doctor."

"No surprise there. Did you?"

"Well, no. The thing is, I thought I knew what was wrong with me. Maybe. And I think she did too. At least she had her suspicions."

Outside, a truck slowed. Francis nodded over the squeal of air brakes. The faint smell of burning rubber wafted up from the pavement through the open window. "That's good, isn't it?"

"I'm not finished." She rocked back and forth on the couch. "I thanked her for her concern. I promised I'd see a doctor, work harder, and get my marks back up. But that didn't seem to be enough. My teacher started pacing around the class-room and then she gave me this whole lecture about how I could always talk to her if I needed to blah, blah, blah—and then she handed me a little booklet and said, 'Read it before it's too late.' I was kind of freaked out, so I shoved it into my backpack and got out of there as fast as I could. I guess I kind of forgot about it. Anyway, I didn't look at the booklet until the next night."

By now Francis was curious. "And? What was in it?"

"Here—read it for yourself." She dug around in her pack and pulled out a rumpled, dog-eared booklet.

Francis took it from her, but didn't immediately look at it. He was terrified. Was she deathly sick? Was that what she was trying to tell him? Was she going to die, like Kevin's dad? He gulped. "I don't know if I can handle this."

"Just read it, Francis. Sometimes we have to handle things that seem impossible. It's called *life*."

Francis's jaw dropped. "You don't have to tell me what life is all about." He pictured Mr. Croyden in his hospital bed waiting to die. *Stop*, he told himself. His eyes wandered to the scratched hardwood floor, the haphazard carpets strewn over it like bandages, the mismatched chairs—all found treasures from garage sales and secondhand stores. Nothing really went together, but it worked—kind of like him and Sawyer, at least he hoped so.

Braced for the worst, he turned over the booklet and began to read, but he got only as far as the title when he had to stop. "What?" Confused, he read it over again and then once more. "I don't understand. It doesn't make sense. Are you sure?" He threw the little book onto the coffee table, as if it might explode in his hands. "This is bullshit."

"I wish. I'm not a hundred percent sure. I've been late before, but never for months."

"But...we only did it that once, the first time, without a... you know...just once. And that was months ago."

"A *condom*. Isn't that the word you're looking for, Francis? And yes, we only did it once without protection, but apparently, once is enough."

"But that was three months ago—and you just figured it out? Jesus!"

Francis retrieved the booklet and turned it over in his hands. *So You Think You Are Pregnant: Options for Teens.*

"It says *options* right in the title. What options? Where is the option page? Jesus!"

"Chill, Francis. I'm not even positive that's the problem." Her scared look spoke differently.

"Have you told anyone else?"

"No—" A light tap on the door interrupted her. "Give me that," she demanded, snatching the booklet away from him. "For now, we'll keep this between ourselves. Promise?"

He thought for a second before he made up his mind. "I guess."

There was another, more persistent knock on the door. "Oh god. Is this What's His Face? Talk about bad timing."

Sawyer stood. "His name is Jack, and don't start in on him again. You can be so immature sometimes."

"Maybe that's because I *am* immature. In case you forgot, I'm fifteen years old. I'm a kid, and I'm not having a kid, no matter what you say. And don't take this wrong, but if you are actually pregnant, how do you know the kid is mine? For all I know, your precious Jack is the father."

"Pardon me?" Sawyer hissed. The blood drained from her face. "Did you just say what I think you said? You shit!" She pointed to the door. "Go. Go now."

Francis recoiled in the face of her fury. "But…it's a fair question."

"Get out," she whispered, her eyes welling up. "Get out. I never, ever want to see you again."

"Now who is the immature one?" He knew he was being unreasonable, but he didn't care. "Have it your way, but like

I said, for all I know, Jack is the father, unless you can prove otherwise. Talk to *him* about it!"

In a flash of anger, he jumped up from the couch and stormed to the door. He yanked it open only to find himself face-to-face with a tall, reed-thin boy dressed in extremely skinny and extremely cool black jeans, a purple tailored button-down shirt, and pointy-toed ebony shoes. He was older than Francis and somehow managed to look both sophisticated and streetwise at the same time. His hair, parted on the right side, fell to his shoulders in all the colors of the rainbow. He smelled faintly of cigarette smoke and coffee.

"You!" Francis roared. He wanted to punch his lights out, but Jack was tall and, despite his slight build, he had a strong, tough look about him that made Francis think twice about hitting him.

Startled, the boy took a step back. "If by 'you,' you mean Jack Meneer, that's me." He looked Francis up and down and nodded slowly. "I take it you're Francis."

"Screw you," Francis muttered.

"Nice to meet you too."

"Don't bother, Jack," Sawyer called from inside the apartment. "Francis is just on his way out."

"True that," Francis snapped. He glowered at his rival.

Jack met his gaze unblinkingly. "Looks like I've come at a bad time."

Francis pushed past him as Sawyer appeared in the doorway. "Actually, Jack, your timing is perfect. Come in." She pulled the boy into the apartment and slammed the door, leaving Francis alone in the hall.

Furious, he slammed his hand against the wall. "Shit. Shit, shit, shit!"

He plunged down the stairs and ducked out onto the rain-drenched street, breaking into a sprint. He ran until the stitch in his side felt like a deep knife wound. His breathing came in short, shallow gasps, but still his anger prevailed. When he finally stumbled up into a bus, the driver greeted him with a concerned "You okay, son?"

Francis fumbled for his bus pass.

"Don't worry about that," the driver said, waving him on.

He played the scene at Sawyer's place over and over again in his mind on the long ride home. He'd never seen Sawyer so angry. At one point, he almost called her, but he stopped himself. What point would there be in talking to her until she'd cooled off? Actually, he corrected himself, there was no point in talking to her at all if she couldn't or wouldn't be honest with him. His questions were legit. Jack could easily be the father of the baby, if there was a baby at all. Who was to say she wasn't lying about the whole thing? He'd heard about stuff like that before.

And what about Jack? He knew a bit about him; the dude worked full-time at a coffee shop—The Grinder—that's where Sawyer had met him. He lived in a dingy basement suite with no windows. So, either he had no parents or he was old enough to live on his own. Which meant he'd either finished university or had never gone. In the end, Francis realized he didn't know much at all and certainly nothing helpful.

By the time he got home, his mood had worsened. Ralph

was waiting for him at his usual spot on the mat inside the front door. When Francis walked past him without even a pat on the head, the dog tucked his tail between his legs and let out a little cry. Francis didn't care. He snapped at the twins and grunted at his mother when she asked him about his day. "I can see you're still angry with your father," she conjectured.

Good! Let her think that, because if she knew the real reason for his foul mood, she'd never forgive him. The thought of it turned his stomach. He imagined her dumbfounded response: *I knew I didn't like that girl. We are so disappointed in you!*

At dinner, Francis sat in angry silence, pushing his food around his plate, before he pleaded a stomachache and asked to be excused. With a skeptical look, his mom waved him away. Whether she'd bought it or not meant nothing to him. He had bigger problems. Lying on his bed, headphones on, he struggled to put those problems into context. So what if he never saw Sawyer again? So what if she had another boyfriend? He didn't give a damn about her father or her life in London or her stupid friend Jack. And even if it was true, and she was pregnant, he didn't give a damn about that either, because if it were true, his life would be over.

And if it were true, it was her fault; she was the experienced one. She was the girl. The whole thing had been her idea. She should have taken care of the birth control.

At least, that's what he told himself as he tossed and turned all night.

By morning, Francis was in worse shape. Lack of sleep did nothing to improve his mood throughout the day. School was a write-off. As the week progressed, he felt himself withdrawing from his world. Every so often, he caught Kevin eyeing him warily, but Kevin's attempts to talk to him were futile. Eventually, to Francis's relief, he gave up.

For the first time ever, Francis skipped soccer practice. He didn't even bother to inform Coach. That afternoon, Kevin bombarded him with text messages, so he turned off his phone, but not before he sent him a curt text: *Leave me alone. I'm a shitty friend, and that's how it is right now.*

His dark mood took a toll on his mom, but Francis didn't have the energy to worry about her or the twins, who had taken to tiptoeing around his black temper with hurt looks on their small faces. For the sixth night in a row, Francis skipped dinner and opted instead to lie on his bed with a bag of chips and stare at the cracks in the ceiling while his mind looped back to his conversation with Sawyer.

I think I'm pregnant.

So, you think you might be three months pregnant and you just figured it out?

Sawyer hadn't once called or texted him. He couldn't blame her, not really, after what he'd said and how he'd acted.

Still, he was terrified and maintained, privately, that it was all a lie.

What are my options? he asked himself. *I could run away, or kill myself.* But he knew he didn't have the will or the guts to do either.

Late at night, ten days into his depression, his despondent reflections were interrupted by a soft knock on his bedroom door. He ignored it, but whoever it was, and he knew the answer to that question, was persistent. "Go away, Mom!"

It's not that he hated her. It's just that he couldn't face her anxious questions—not when his betrayal was so complete— good-bye scholarship. It'd kill his parents.

The door slowly opened. "It's not your mom. It's me. Kevin."

"Leave me alone." Francis turned his back on his friend. "I mean it. Eff off."

The door clicked shut, and Francis breathed a sigh of relief and pulled his pillow over his head.

"I'm not gone, asshole."

"Fuck." He rolled over and saw Kevin watching him warily from across the room. His arms were folded and he leaned against the door, his eyes bright with anger and something else: fear.

"I'm not going anywhere until you tell me what's up with you. I can't believe you skipped practice and didn't let Coach know." He crossed the floor in three steps and planted himself at the foot of Francis's bed. "I mean it. I'm not moving until I know what's going on."

"You're being weird."

"It's your girlfriend, isn't it? You guys have broken up. Good. I never liked her, anyway." He took a breath. "Now, that's over. Want to kick the ball around, play some video games?"

"It's worse," Francis squeaked, unable to be anything but relieved at having someone to confess to. "I'm fifteen. Sawyer thinks she is pregnant—almost four months pregnant—not that I get what that means. I'm going to get kicked out of Hudson, lose my scholarship. I'm dead." The words flooded out of him, leaving him exhausted.

He watched as Kevin's eyes grew wide.

"I'm in a world of shit," he added.

"Holy shit. I mean…holy shit." Kevin paced back and forth from the door to the bed. "Seriously, *holy shit.*"

"Yeah. Helpful. But you're right. Holy shit. I think Sawyer and I are broken up. I think she's seeing someone else…but that's the least of my worries right now. I'm dead," he repeated.

Kevin sucked in a mouthful of air. "How can she be pregnant?"

Francis propped himself up on one elbow. "Jesus, Kevin."

His friend's face reddened. "Sorry. And are you sure? You know, that there's something going on with someone else? I mean, that could be good. It could mean…"

Francis rolled off the bed and went over to the window. "I'm not sure of anything—except that I'm dead."

Kevin was as uncomfortable as Francis with this whole exchange. "Has she seen a doctor?"

"I don't know. She kicked me out before we could really talk about it."

"When?"

"Last week, or the week before. I've kind of lost count."

"And you haven't spoken since?"

"Nope. She's pissed, but I'm the one who is screwed. I unfriended her on everything."

"Yeah, tough guy. You're an idiot." Kevin moved to the

window and sighed. "You have to find out the truth; even if you are broken up, you need to know if there is a…well, you need to know."

"How?"

"Face-to-face. I'll go with you. After school tomorrow. Set it up. One way or the other, we've got to get some answers."

"She might not agree to meeting."

"Then it's your job to persuade her."

"I'll try." He rubbed his temples. "How's your dad?"

Kevin bit his top lip. "He's still alive. For now."

Chapter Six

You have reached the end of your first trimester. Congratulations! Your baby is moving in your uterus, although you can't feel it yet. Your baby is growing delicate, pink skin and starting to look more human. Your baby is approximately the size of half a roll of Life Savers.

Excerpt: *From Conception to Birth*

Coach sought Francis out the next day. Though Francis saw that his intentions were good, he couldn't risk confiding in him of all people, so he was evasive when Coach asked, "Is anything wrong?"

"Just a bit of pressure, with school, home, Kevin's dad." Francis hoped this explanation would keep Coach off his back for a while, but he made a note to himself that he needed to pull it together and act like everything was normal.

"I'm here to talk to you whenever you need me," Coach assured him. "And make sure you're at the next practice, or I'll have to bench you and, of course, get in touch with your parents."

At lunchtime, Francis was half-surprised to receive a text from Sawyer in answer to the one he'd sent her in the morning. He'd been doubtful that she'd agree to meet with him and Kevin after school, but she did, though her text message was terse and unfriendly: *Fine, but don't be an asshole, or I'll throw U out again. S.*

Though he was grateful for Kevin's support, he wasn't confident his friend's presence at Sawyer's would change much. Besides, after last night's frank conversation, they were both slightly embarrassed and avoided each other at school.

Francis almost expected Kevin to back out, but when the final bell rang, Francis found Kevin waiting at his locker. "Did you hear from her?"

"Yup. I got a text at lunch. She agreed. So…you're still coming?"

"I said I would," Kevin answered, although he looked like he was having second thoughts.

They spoke little to each other on the bus to the East Side. Both were anxious, but they kept their misgivings to themselves until they were standing outside Sawyer's door. "This whole thing," Kevin muttered, "is super weird."

"We could leave," Francis suggested hopefully.

Kevin's answer was to knock on the door. "Nope," he said with a wry smile. "We're here now."

"Enter." Sawyer's voice came through the door. She greeted Francis coolly but was pleasant to Kevin. "Hey, it's good to see you. Thanks for bringing Francis over. I knew he wouldn't have come alone. Every couple needs a Tiresias to help out now and again."

"Yeah. Whatever." Kevin buried his hands deep in the pockets of his flannel school pants. "No problem," he stammered. It wasn't hard to tell he'd lost his nerve. Or that he didn't have a clue who or what she meant by Tiresias. Francis didn't either, and he didn't ask for clarification.

He saw Kevin's eyes travel around the apartment, full of curiosity. "Different" was all he managed after some observation, not looking at her.

Francis winced, but Sawyer didn't react.

Francis studied her carefully out of the corner of his eyes. She was wearing her usual black leggings and a man's plaid shirt that fell to just above her knees. She didn't look like a girl who might be pregnant—not fat or anything. Her feet were bare, and the lime-green polish on her toenails was chipped. Her whole attitude screamed casual, but the way she twirled her long hair in nervous fingers was a dead giveaway; she was tense.

She stepped aside. "I'm making hot chocolate. Do you want some?"

"Sure," said Kevin. "Sounds good."

Sawyer led them into the kitchen, where she chatted to Kevin while she stirred the dark chocolate chunks into the hot milk. Francis saw that Kevin was still pretty tongue-tied, as he struggled for something to say, sitting there awkwardly at the small table. Despite all of his bravado, girls were foreign to him too. When Sawyer asked him how his dad was doing, he hid his pain with a nonchalant shrug. "The same. Not good."

"I'm sorry. I hear he's a stand-up guy." With a bright smile, she changed the subject. "Grab some mugs from the cupboard above your head. We'll drink this at the table."

In spite of Sawyer's efforts at politeness, it felt like a meeting, not three friends getting together for an after-school snack. Still, Francis credited his friend for doing his best to play along, praising Sawyer's hot chocolate. "This is amazing. The only time I've had hot chocolate this good was in Italy."

Francis braced himself for a sarcastic response from Sawyer as he sat down to join them, but she just nodded politely and explained in great detail how it was done. Kevin feigned interest. It seemed they liked each other. Once, that would have meant something to Francis. Not anymore.

It was Sawyer who brought an end to the small talk. With an apologetic nod to Kevin, she said, "We need to straighten out some misunderstandings. That's what you're here for, right? Helping Francis to not be a jerk?"

"Hey," Francis interjected, but Kevin cut him off with a hostile frown. "I think Francis has something to say first, don't you, Francis?"

"Yeah." Francis inhaled; they'd talked about this last night. He hadn't wanted to agree to it, and he didn't want to now, but he knew he had to trust someone, and Kevin was that someone. "Sorry I was a jerk the other day when you told me, you know—"

She cut him off. "Apology accepted. I could have been a little more tactful too. I've had a bit more time than you to grow used to the idea of being pregnant…I should let you know, though; I've invited Jack to join us. I need someone on my team too." She glanced up at the kitchen clock. "He's a bit late, but he'll be here."

"That makes sense," Kevin agreed before Francis lost his temper. "I mean, he's your friend, right?"

Sawyer shot him a grateful smile just as there was a loud knock on the door. "It's open," she yelled. "Francis, remember you promised not to be a jerk. This thing is bigger than us now."

When Jack walked in, he wore the same skinny jeans and purple shirt as the other day, but he didn't look rumpled. Kevin's eyes widened. The older boy carried a backpack and two plastic bags, which he dumped unceremoniously on the floor by the couch.

Francis kicked his friend under the table. *Stop staring*, he tried to tell him. But Kevin couldn't. Whether Jack didn't notice or didn't care was anyone's guess. He ignored Francis and Kevin entirely, and grimaced at Sawyer. "Sorry I'm late. I've got some bad news."

Sawyer's forehead creased. "Come and sit. What's going on? You okay?"

Francis braced his legs against the table. This was too much. *Poor Jack. Always Jack.*

Jack pulled a cigarette out from behind his ear, put the

end in his mouth, frowned, and then put it back. "I'm kicked out. I was hoping I could stay with you for a few days until I find another place."

This was more than Francis could handle. "I bet you were." He flew out of his chair and it crashed to the floor. "How convenient."

"Whoa." Jack took an exaggerated step back. "Grow up. Let's not start that crap again," he said. "Are you *ever* normal?"

Kevin stood up too and clamped his hand down on Francis's shoulder. "Sit back down."

Francis sat down and pushed Kevin's hand away. "Leave me alone."

With a wave of his hand, Jack dismissed Francis and concentrated on Sawyer. "I'm sorry about this. All of it."

"Don't be." She gnawed on her fingernail. "Ignore him. You are always welcome here. Especially if you're in trouble."

"I know, and I thank you." Jack pulled her into a big bear hug.

Francis watched them, his hands clasped together under the table. He counted slowly to ten in his head. It took that long for the embrace to end. When it did, Kevin let out a loud breath.

"So tell me what happened," Sawyer encouraged. "But first, you've met Francis, and this is his friend Kevin. We're all here now."

Kevin stood and they shook hands.

"You're not going to try and kill me too, are you?" Jack teased.

Kevin grinned. "Nah."

"I'm hot and sticky," Jack apologized. "Rough shift. Nonstop double-shot, low-fat, skinny mochas all afternoon."

"You have a job and go to school?" Kevin asked.

"Yeah. I'm a bit older than you guys. You're what—fifteen?"

"In a month," said Kevin. "But Francis already had his birthday."

Jack shook his head in Sawyer's direction. "Cradle robber!"

She scrunched her nose at him. "Old man. Besides, I thought Francis was very mature for his age. Now I'm not so sure."

Francis rubbed his temples, but managed to stay silent.

"So, how are you doing today? You look a little green," Jack said, switching subjects. He took Sawyer's hand. "Poor you."

Sawyer slumped in her seat. "A bit better now that you're here, but not great."

"For Christ's sake," Francis muttered. "Should we leave now?"

A warning look from Jack shut him up.

"So, you're homeless. That sucks." Sawyer's eyes softened.

"It does. Do you think your mom will be okay with me sleeping on the couch for a few days?"

"Yes. She loves you almost as much as I do." She touched his arm gently. "Why'd you get kicked out of your apartment?"

"Apartment?" Jack scoffed. "You mean that shit-hole cellar room with no windows?"

"You can stay here for as long as you like. Like I said, Mom loves you. She thinks you are a good influence on me."

Francis rocked his chair on its back legs. "As opposed to me," he sneered.

Kevin cleared his throat. Francis had every right to be upset. Jack was crossing a line, but he couldn't quite put his finger on what that line was. His friend was right; they were way too close. If he didn't intervene, Francis would lose it for sure. "Uh, if we could get back to the reason we're all here and deal with Jack's shit later?"

"No. Let's go." Francis had had enough. "We'll talk some other time, Sawyer. Maybe when your friend gets his life sorted out and it's not all about him."

"Enough, Francis." Sawyer turned to stare at him. "Kevin's right. We need to talk about this…this…well, about me and…"

Nobody spoke. At last Jack broke the silence. "I'm sorry. Francis has a point. It's my fault you got off-track. So, I'll say what we're all thinking: Sawyer, you need to see a doctor. Nothing can be confirmed until you do."

"What I need is to go back to London," Sawyer whispered. "Put this all behind me." She looked pointedly at Francis again.

"No." Jack sounded exasperated Francis thought, and he understood why. "I've told you before. London is just a place. Home is where you are surrounded by people you love. Home is here. Right here!"

"True that," Kevin said softly. He was thinking about his dad. "Jack is right. Home is about people, not places."

"Thanks, Kevin." The older boy helped himself to a sip of Sawyer's hot chocolate. "I know I'm right. Sawyer, you're the color of old oatmeal and your stomach is in knots. You've got zero energy, and you're bitchy as hell. You're convinced you're pregnant, but you don't know for sure. There is a walk-in clinic two blocks away. Let's go now. No appointment necessary."

"Now? Are you out of your mind?"

"Now. Why not? We're all here. Otherwise, we're just going to sit around until Francis kills me." When nobody laughed, he added "Joke."

"Fine," Sawyer agreed reluctantly. "I'll go, but only if you shut up."

"Great." Francis leapt out of his seat. "Kevin and I will head home. Sawyer, text me when you find out, if you want to—no pressure—after all, you have Jack."

"I won't have to text you." Sawyer's eyes challenged him. "We're all going. You too."

"Oh, I don't think so. That's nuts. We can't all go."

She got up and tossed him his coat. "Yes, we can. And I don't care how you feel about it. Let's go. I just want to get this over with."

"What? Me too?"

"Yes, you too, Kevin. Someone has to control Francis."

"Maybe I can help with that." Jack stepped between Francis and Sawyer. "With a little bit of truth. If he'll listen. I'm only going to say this once. There is nothing, I repeat, nothing going on between Sawyer and me." His voice was low and rough. "Except that we're friends, and that's it."

"Sure." Francis didn't believe a word of it, but Jack's size and tone intimidated him. "Of course I believe you. I mean, of course this is all my fault."

"Lose the sarcasm, kid." Jack took a step closer to Francis, so close that Francis could feel his breath on his cheeks. "You're just a kid. Just a stupid kid. I tried. Now let's go, because if

Sawyer changes her mind, I'm going to hold you responsible. And you are coming with us, even if I have to knock you out and carry you to the clinic."

"Knock it off, Jack." Sawyer took his arm.

"I just want to be clear that we're all going to the clinic together."

"Yeah," agreed Kevin, too quickly. "Good idea."

Sawyer laughed. "I'm so glad you came today."

Kevin blushed and headed for the door. Francis trailed behind him, wishing he were a bit bigger and a lot braver.

They headed off down the street in pairs; Jack and Sawyer led the way. The first fat raindrops bounced off the pavement as they ducked into the clinic. To everyone's relief, the waiting room sat empty. Sawyer went straight to the reception desk; the boys hung back. When Jack sat down, Francis took a seat on the other side of the room.

"Yes?" The receptionist eyed Sawyer. "What can I do for you?"

"I'd like to see a doctor."

"All four of you?"

"No." Sawyer shook her head. "I need to see a doctor, and these are my friends."

"Okay. Lucky for you we are not very busy right now, but you'll have to fill out these forms." She glanced at her computer screen. "Dr. Chung will be available in about fifteen minutes." She handed Sawyer a clipboard, thick with papers and a pen.

"Thanks." Sawyer made her way back to where Jack sat. "Look at this! I have to fill out a million forms. The doctor will ask me the same questions all over again when I go in. I can't believe you are forcing me to do this. What a waste of time." Her voice trembled.

"It doesn't have to be." Jack grinned. "We could make it fun. What if we give bogus answers? I'll bet you she never reads the forms. Five bucks says the doctor won't even notice."

"I like it," Kevin said. He ignored Francis's glare and crossed the room. Francis knew he had to follow or look like a real jerk.

Sure enough, creating a make-believe history turned out to be an excellent time-killer and the receptionist had to call Sawyer's name twice before they heard her.

Sawyer winked at Jack and handed the clipboard back to the receptionist. "All done. We've answered every question, but if you need clarification, ask him." She leaned down and kissed Jack. "Wish me luck."

"You don't need luck; you need Gravol." He pulled out his phone. "Don't worry, I've got a new game. I'm not going anywhere."

He managed to act nonchalant until she disappeared into the exam room, then he let out a long sigh. "What a mess," he said to no one in particular. "Her, my stupid father, everything."

Francis nodded. "It's a mess, all right."

They sat there for a long time, nearly half an hour, until the receptionist spoke again. "If Jack and Francis could follow me, please. The doctor would like to see both of you."

The look of pure relief that washed over Kevin's face made Francis smile, despite the circumstances.

"Is she okay?" Jack wanted to know.

The receptionist's gaze was practiced, measured. "There is nothing seriously wrong with your friend, except that," she said, grinning, and glanced at the chart in her hand. "She looks really good for a forty-year-old who has had heart surgery, TB, and, oh, I love this one, a sex change."

"Sorry." Jack grinned sheepishly. "We were just trying to cheer her up."

"Follow me." She led the boys to the door of the examination room. "Go on in," she said.

The room was small and brightly lit. Sawyer sat on the examination table, fully dressed in her usual leggings and purple sweater. The doctor gave them both a welcoming smile. "Please sit."

"Hey," Jack said to Sawyer. "All good?"

"Yeah," Francis repeated, wishing he had asked first. "All good?"

Sawyer chewed on her fingernail. Her eyes were red and a line of mascara ran down her cheek. She looked at the doctor. "She'll tell you."

"Hello. I'm Dr. Chung." The doctor was a trim woman with intelligent eyes.

"I'm Jack, and this is Francis," explained Jack.

"It's complicated," added Sawyer.

Dr. Chung nodded with professional coolness. "It always is. Have a seat, both of you."

The doctor studied each boy in turn. "Your friend is not ill. However, she is expecting a baby." She turned to Sawyer. "So, young lady, which one is the father, or do you know?"

The blood drained from Francis's face, and he put his head between his knees and groaned. This wasn't going to go over well.

"Of course I know," Sawyer shrieked. "It's not like that. You've got it wrong."

The doctor gave her a searching look. "If it's not like that, how exactly is it? Why are there two boys in this room?"

"Jack is my best friend and the other one, well…he's the other one, and he's the father."

"Well, you'll have to sort that out. 'Man up' is the expression, I believe. In the meantime, Sawyer has requested that both of you be here, and that's fine with me. She's asked that I confirm to both of you that she is, indeed, pregnant."

Francis raised his head. "With a baby?"

"No, with an alien," Jack snorted.

"To continue," Dr. Chung said, ignoring them both, "we will do an ultrasound to confirm the dates."

"You little shit." Jack raised his fist at Francis. "I could smash your face."

"Or not." Dr. Chung pursed her lips. "I'll call security if I have to."

"No, it's okay," Jack said apologetically. "Like she said, there's no way I could be the father, despite what Francis thinks."

"BS," retorted Francis.

"Enough!" intervened Dr. Chung. "I'm not concerned about who the father is right now. If it comes to it, we can do a paternity test. But what does concern me is that Sawyer is quite pregnant. Just under four months. That means her choices are somewhat narrowed down."

"Four months!" Jack stared at Francis, then at Sawyer. "Idiots," he mumbled under his breath. "I told you to go to the doctor sooner."

"I'm sorry," Sawyer blurted out. "I was scared."

"Sawyer," the doctor interrupted again, "is also anemic and underweight. Her baby is not getting the nourishment it needs, and neither is she."

"Mom is always at work. I get tired of cooking and shopping."

"Yes, well, I've prescribed prenatal vitamins, iron pills, and I strongly suggest she stop eating dinner at the corner store."

"That's what I said," offered Francis, finally finding his voice.

"You've been eating at Joe's?" Jack frowned. "God, no wonder you're anemic. No wonder you feel sick!"

"Joe's is convenient," Sawyer defended. "Hence the name 'convenience store.'"

Dr. Chung cleared her throat. "She feels sick because she has morning sickness. It's perfectly common and the least of her worries. The good news is, the nausea should disappear, as it generally does after the first three or four months. Here's a prescription. Be sure to fill this as soon as you leave here. Sawyer, I'll need to see you a week from now, when you've had time to digest this news. Oh, and start eating food that's good for you. And make sure you read this—actually, that goes for all of you. Everything you need to know you'll find in here, but if you have any questions, any cramping or any bleeding, call the clinic. We're open seven days a week."

"Okay." Sawyer climbed down off the table. "Come on, you guys." She sounded tired.

"One more thing, Sawyer." Dr. Chung's voice was grave. "I want you to give serious thought to what you want to do. You do have options, but for now all you have to do is to take care of yourself—and talk to your mother. I'll see you in a week's time."

They left the exam room together. Kevin raised his eyebrows when he saw his friend. "Not good," Francis mouthed. He felt sick. How was he going to explain this to his parents? Maybe he wouldn't have to.

Outside the clinic, they huddled together. Sawyer clutched the prescription in her hand. "I'm glad you came," she said to Francis. "I was afraid you wouldn't."

Jack pulled out a pack of cigarettes and lit one. "He would have had to answer to me if he no-showed." He scowled at Francis. "This is your fault as much as it is hers." He took a drag, the smoke filling his lungs, and exhaled slowly. "God, I can't believe this is happening."

For once he spoke for all of them.

Kevin took hold of Francis's arm. "If it's okay with you guys, I think we're going to head home. I think Francis needs some time to digest this."

"Uh-huh." Francis was still reeling from the confirmation of his worst nightmare. All he could think was, maybe he'd get away with it. Maybe his parents wouldn't have to know. "I'm dead," he said to nobody in particular.

"I'm glad you came, both of you." Sawyer pushed a brochure toward Francis. Dr. Chung said you have to read this. Go home and read it and then we'll talk. And I mean it: Thanks for coming. It's not good, but it's better if I have you."

"Come on. We've got a prescription to fill." Jack shot Francis a warning look. "Don't disappear again," he threatened. "She needs you."

Kevin stepped toward Jack. "Back off. Do you think this is easy for him?" Kevin was much smaller than Jack, and his unexpected aggression shocked them all.

"Take it easy, bro." Jack held up his hands. "Just make sure your friend does his homework. Whatever happens is going to be a group decision. It can't all be on Sawyer's shoulders."

"Got it. Come on, Francis. We've got a bus to catch."

Francis, too shocked to do anything except follow Kevin's lead, obeyed. Once on the bus, he pulled out the pamphlet Sawyer had given him: *From Conception to Birth*. The more he read, the worse he felt.

So you're having a baby—those five words made the whole situation horribly real, but the following explanations drove another terrible truth home:

> You may need some time to think about your
> choices. Counseling may help you to decide
> what is best for you. If you're comfortable,
> you can start by talking with your doctor.
> Family planning clinics also offer counseling
> to help you decide what is best for you. You

may also want to talk with someone close to you who understands how pregnancy and raising a child would affect your life. Carefully think through your choices, which are to:

- Have a baby, and support and raise your child to adulthood.

- Have a baby, and place the baby for adoption.

- Have an abortion.

"Do you think that means it's too late to, you know, abort the baby?" Kevin wondered out loud.

"How the eff should I know? And it's not human. It's not a baby. It's a fetus."

"Well, you *should* know. That's your whole problem," Kevin snapped. "You're lazy. It's time you started educating yourself and stopped blaming your girlfriend. It takes two to make a kid."

"Whose side are you on, anyway? How was I supposed to know this would happen?"

"You know, Francis, you *can* be a jerk sometimes. First you jump to conclusions, then you blame Sawyer, you don't listen, and when you do, you don't accept anything. News flash! Shit happens in life. You have to learn to deal with it. And while we're on the subject, I was in the same sex-ed class as you, so don't give me that BS about just being some poor, ignorant kid."

"Easy for you to say. You don't have anything to worry about. I'd change places with you in a second, and then we'd see how great you are at handling shit."

As soon as the words were out of his mouth, Francis regretted them, but he didn't take them back. Instead, he said, "I never thought I'd hear myself say this, but I hope Jack is the dad. Not me."

Chapter Seven

By the fourth month, your baby weighs around 1.6 ounces (45g) and is about 4 inches (10cm) long. Its arms, legs, hands, and feet are very distinct. The nervous system is developed and the muscles are forming so the fetus begins to move. The movements are very small but quite sudden.

Excerpt: *From Conception to Birth*

The wet weather had not subsided by the end of the week, nor had Francis's dark mood. It didn't help when he left school on a gloomy Friday afternoon and spotted Jack huddled beneath a tattered umbrella under the cheerless December sky. *Now what?* he griped to himself.

Jack looked nervous. He hovered at the edge of the wide,

tree-lined cobblestone driveway and shuffled from foot to foot. Francis couldn't tell if he was just cold, or on edge. He hoped the latter. In his dark clothes, Jack brought to mind a raven stuck in an enclosure of peacocks. Jack stood out.

On closer observation, Francis saw that unease radiated off him as he eyed the flow of uniformed boys pouring out of the school, full of anticipation for the weekend that lay ahead, while their well-dressed mothers talked about spa days and dinners out and exotic trips.

Obviously, he was looking for Francis in the crowd. But he'd be hard to pick out because all the boys wore a uniform— pressed, gray flannel pants, blue ties, and gray blazers that sported yellow-and-red crests. As they poured out into the wet, sad afternoon, some threw curious glances at Jack, but most ignored him. Francis didn't have that choice. He skirted the cluster of parents and loyal nannies waiting patiently for their charges at the bottom of the stone staircase and approached from behind so that Jack wouldn't have the advantage of see- ing him first.

He had no doubt about what Jack was after. It had been nearly a week since he'd spoken to Sawyer, longer since he'd seen her, a lot longer. Although she'd made many attempts to contact him, texting and calling daily, he'd ignored every one. It wasn't that he was a jerk or that he was angry with her. No. The truth was, he just couldn't deal with the whole baby thing. He'd justified his behavior in a million different ways, but in the end, he was forced to admit that he was a shit and a coward, and so be it.

Besides, hadn't Sawyer chosen Jack over him? Wasn't he sleeping under the same roof as her every night? He sighed and edged closer to Jack, his whole body on alert.

Jack was soaked. He'd been waiting for more than forty-five minutes for the final bell that signaled the end of the school day, unaware that private schools got out later than public schools.

Francis thought about sneaking out the back entrance, but knew this was probably a confrontation he couldn't avoid. Jack wouldn't stop looking for him until he'd found him. *At least I have surprise on my side*, he mused as he reached out and tapped Jack on the shoulder. "What are you doing here?" He did his best to sound menacing. Jack swung around, fists up, but when he saw Francis, a look of relief flashed in his eyes. "You shouldn't sneak up on people like that. You're liable to get hurt."

"Yeah, and you shouldn't stalk people. You might get hurt too," Francis retorted.

"Relax, Francis. I'm not here to cause trouble." He pointed at the school motto emblazed on Francis's jacket. *Hudson Preparatory School. Strive to be your best.* "Nice sentiment. You should try to live up to it."

"Why are you here? Oh, let me guess: Sawyer sent you?"

"Not exactly." Jack sighed. "She'd kill me if she had any idea." He seemed sincere and a bit nervous, which surprised Francis and made him feel like he had the advantage for once.

Francis noticed they'd drawn the attention of a few kids.

"Let's get out of here." He started to walk toward the gates, but Jack stayed put.

"Come on. We can walk and talk."

"What's the hurry? Are you ashamed to be seen with a guy like me?"

"You're trespassing. I could call security."

"Is that the best you've got?"

"We have nothing to talk about." Francis kept walking.

Jack shook his head. "All right. Have it your way, but you should know that it cost me fifteen bucks for a cab to get here and I'm going to be late for work. I'm not leaving until I've said what I came to say." He paused. "Nice school, by the way," he added.

"I'm a scholarship student," Francis defended.

"Yeah. I heard. One thing's for sure—I couldn't have survived in a school without girls."

"It's not as bad as you might think."

"It is. Boys can be assholes. And then they grow into asshole men."

"Thanks for that. Asshole men that steal other guys' girlfriends, you mean?"

Jack's eyes narrowed, but he refused to rise to the bait. "Like I said, Sawyer would kill me if she knew I was here, but there's something you need to know."

"Yeah, well, this better be good. I've got soccer practice and I can't be late again."

They stopped walking and ducked under the broad leaves of an old oak tree. Francis pulled his collar up, but the rain was relentless. Jack's umbrella threatened to turn inside out with one more gust of wind. They'd reached a standoff. "Can we get on with this?" Francis said.

"Sure, but like I said, we have to keep this between us. Sawyer would be choked if she knew I were here."

"We're not exactly talking these days," Francis admitted.

"That's because you've blocked her in every way possible."

"I don't see how that's any of your business."

"I'm not here to argue with you."

"So why *are* you here, then?"

"Because you're being a jerk and she needs you right now."

"She does? Why? Are you not enough for her?" What right did this guy have to call him a jerk? "What the hell is your problem?"

"I've got a shitload of problems," Jack exploded. He ticked them off with his fingers. "Let's see. I've got nowhere to live, which you might not think is such a big deal, 'cause in my position, you'd probably just check into the nearest hotel, and, let's see…I'm living paycheck to paycheck. I guess a rich kid like you never has to think about money, though. Plus, I've got you assuming something that's all bullshit. I'm not interested in Sawyer that way. You are the dad. Not me. Don't take my word for it. Take the blood test. Are all rich kids this stubborn?"

Jack's observations stunned Francis. Was this how strangers saw him—a spoiled kid with no worries in the world? "Dude, like I told you, I'm on a scholarship here. I'm not rich, so screw you. That chip on your shoulder is going to kill you.

And Sawyer is pregnant and suddenly you're not interested in her 'that way'? Give me a fucking break. You can't pin this on me. I'm not going to fuck up my whole life to save your ass."

Jack shook his head in disgust. "The baby is not mine," he said, slowly emphasizing each word. "Not mine," he repeated, just in case Francis was as stupid as he was acting. "And by the way, have you ever heard of protection, shithead?"

"Hey. I don't need a self-righteous lecture on birth control, especially from you. Besides, we only did it once without protection."

"You're such an ass," Jack observed.

"So, Jack. Tell me. What makes you so certain that you're not the father? I know you've slept together, so don't try to deny it. She already admitted that I wasn't the first guy she'd slept with."

Jack stopped. He placed both hands on Francis's chest and pushed him—hard.

Francis fell backward. "You'll regret that," he threatened as he struggled to find his footing on the slick sidewalk.

"Listen to me! I can assure you, Sawyer and I are the best of friends, and yes, we've known each other since she moved here. I can also attest that we've slept in the same bed many times and I've spent lots of nights on her sofa. However, we have never, ever, ever had sex."

"And you expect me to believe that?"

"Yeah, I do. You see, Francis, there's something you should know about me."

"I can hardly wait."

Jack regarded Francis unflinchingly. "I'd rather sleep with you."

Francis's jaw dropped. "What the fuck? You better watch what you are saying."

"Chill, Francis. I'm gay." Jack crossed his arms across his chest. "As in, I don't like girls that way."

Francis froze, but he still didn't believe Jack. "I think you're full of shit. I would have noticed."

Jack scowled. "That's what all the straight guys who have no gaydar say."

"Why didn't Sawyer tell me, then?" Francis demanded.

"Because it didn't matter. Because it was none of your bloody business. Until now." Jack spun around. "Screw you. I'm done here. I'll see you later. And don't tell Sawyer I talked to you, or I'll do more than just shove you to the ground. Act like a man. Call her."

"I'm not making any promises." Stunned, Francis remained rooted to the sidewalk long after Jack marched away. He didn't want to believe a word Jack said, but he sensed the truth. "Shit," he said, his mind reeling. "Double shit!" Just like that, his whole world had spun out of control.

He had only a few minutes to get to practice. He sprinted down the street and arrived seconds before the whistle blew. He played badly. He fumbled the ball. He found it impossible to concentrate. Sawyer was pregnant. Jack was gay, so he was cleared of all responsibility. He, Francis, was the dad of the kid. *How could there be a kid?* he asked himself for the hundredth time. They'd done it only once without a condom. He stared up at the angry sky and thought about how he'd been so jealous of Jack. Crap! He'd made a complete fool of himself. "God," he muttered to himself. "I am such a loser." The ball sailed over his head and landed between the goalposts. "Sloan!" Coach's angry whistle brought him back to the present. "Sloan! Either get your head into the game or get off the field and go home. Sloan! Can you hear me?"

"Yes, Coach. Sorry, Coach." Francis kicked the ball out of the goal to his forward. It curved and went out of bounds. "I'll focus. I promise."

"Nope. Too late for sorry. Pack up your stuff and get out of the goal before I bench you for a game."

Maybe the worst thing about getting kicked off the field was sitting in the cold and watching his teammates play. Yet he caught an unexpected break from the guys; they left him alone. He would almost have preferred snide comments to awkward silences and averted eyes. Even Kevin stayed silent as Francis trotted to the sidelines and removed his cleats. He kept his eyes on the practice while his mind explored the mess he'd made of his life.

And if Jack was right, Sawyer's life too.

At halftime, he braced himself for the lecture. Instead, Coach gave him a fatherly thump on the shoulder. "A word," he said, drawing him away from the other boys.

"I'm sorry—" Francis began.

Coach ignored him. "Sloan, I know Croyden is your best friend, and I know you're close to his family," he said gruffly. He gestured toward the rest of the team. "The boys reminded me that you're going through a tough time, supporting Kevin. Take a few days. Do what you have to do to help Kevin, and come back when you're ready." He eyed Francis expectantly. "Deal?"

"Deal," Francis muttered, hating to use Kevin's situation as an excuse. He was a fraud on top of everything else.

"Then stop looking so glum. Shape up. I'll see you back out here in better form—sooner, I hope, rather than later."

Francis walked slowly home, his mind reeling.

When he stumbled in, he found his mom curled up on the couch reading. "Hi, honey. You're home early." She put down her book and studied him. "Are you okay?" Francis answered her question with one of his own. "Where are the Terrible Twins?" He wanted to get down on the floor and wrestle with them as if nothing had changed in his world.

"They've got a playdate. Peace reigns in the Sloan household for a few hours." She smiled weakly. "Honey?"

He suddenly missed his father. "When's Dad home?"

"Tomorrow, but can't I help out?"

"I'm okay," Francis fibbed, forcing his lips to curl up in a smile. He didn't think he'd fooled her, though.

Her brow crinkled. "How was practice?"

"I got kicked off the field."

"Well, that's a first," she said worriedly. "What did you do?"

"I couldn't concentrate." To his surprise, his eyes welled up. He swallowed hard. "I've got a lot on my mind. You know, Kevin's dad…"

"Aw, honey."

"I'm going to take a shower and sleep for a while."

"No snack?"

"Not hungry. I just need to chill, okay?"

"Sure."

At least he'd avoided the usual inquisition. He fell onto his bed and fixed his eyes on the ceiling. *I need someone to talk to.* He couldn't confide in his mom. If only his dad wasn't on the other side of the world. He couldn't call him; some things couldn't be said over the phone. *How am I going to tell them about Sawyer's pregnancy?* Just thinking about that conversation made him sick. Once, he could have counted on Kevin, but not now. He had his own problems to deal with. What about calling Sawyer? No way. He'd rather chew on broken glass than go crawling to her. *After all, she pushed me into having sex in the first place, didn't she? It was her responsibility to be on the pill, not mine…I don't really believe that.* One thing he did believe: He'd screwed up badly.

So that left Jack. Jack was pissed at him, but he cared about Sawyer, and Jack might be helpful. He'd never had a gay friend. Would it look like a come-on? *Jesus, Francis. Get a grip. Call him. There's nobody else.*

When Sawyer had introduced them, she'd used his last name. It began with an *M.* Mandor? Mundy? Meneer…that was it! He grabbed his tablet and found eighteen Meneers in Canada 411. Hell, why not try them all?

He struck out on the first, but got lucky on the second call. A gruff voice snarled, "Yeah."

"Hello. Is this Mr. Meneer?"

"Who wants to know?"

"Um, I'm actually looking for Jack. Jack Meneer. I know he's not there, but I need his cell number."

"You his boyfriend?"

"Uh…no. I'm his boss at work. He forgot his…his wallet here, and this is the only number I have for him."

The guy on the other end of the line coughed, a phlegmy smoker's hack. "I haven't seen Jack for a month. I kicked his sorry ass out. No fags in this house."

"Mr. Meneer. Sir. Do you know Jack's cell number?"

Pause. Francis met the silence with silence. Mr. Meneer cleared his throat. "What the hell—555-987-0987."

"Thank you."

A click and then the dial tone. Francis stared at the phone. What a creep. Before he could change his mind, he dialed the number. After four rings, he heard Jack's familiar voice. "This is an answering machine. You know what to do."

"Jack, Francis here. Uh, can you call me?"

Jack called as soon as his shift ended. "I'm on my way to Sawyer's. Did you talk to her yet?"

"No," Francis admitted. "I'd like to talk to you first."

"Sure. Is there any point in asking you why?" He sounded slightly suspicious. "Okay, I can be on your side of town tomorrow afternoon. Your place. Where do you live?"

Francis paused. He'd thought they would meet somewhere else, not at his house. If he suggested that now, Jack would be insulted and he'd have every right to be, so he gave his address.

"Got it. I'll be there between five and six, and Francis, this better be good."

• • •

Francis felt better after his phone call to Jack the night before. He knew his dad would be home today and that helped his spirits. For the first night in weeks, he had slept well. When his dad walked in the front door, lugging his bags, Devon and Nate bowled him over in their excitement.

"Daddy!" they shouted. "Daddy!" He swept them up into his big arms. "Bike ride in ten minutes, boys! Just let me get out of my uniform."

"Yay!" they screamed. "Bike ride and park!" Ralph joined in the chaos, running in circles and barking happily. For a second, for Francis, perched halfway down the stairs, life felt normal. He chuckled. The twins' excitement was infectious.

"What about Francis?" his dad said, spotting him on the step. "What are you up to? Do you want to come with us?"

"Thanks, but I'm going to visit Kevin, and then I've got a friend coming over around five. Can we catch up later?"

"Are you sure? We haven't been riding together for a while."

"It's hardly a bike ride with them, Dad. So, no thanks." He grinned. "But thanks for asking."

"How is Kevin?"

"Not good. I guess Mom told you…"

"If there is anything I can do…" His dad hoisted a twin into each arm.

Francis shook his head. "I wish, but there's nothing anyone can do."

"I know. And I'm sorry."

"Yeah. Me too."

"Okay, if you're sure you don't want to come, we're off like a herd of turtles. Get those helmets on, boys!"

Once the door closed behind them, Francis and his mother breathed a sigh of relief. "I love my boys, but they are exhausting," his mom admitted. "So, who's coming over?"

"A new friend. His name is Jack. I met him through Sawyer."

"You haven't mentioned her for a while."

"We've kind of broken up." He knew he sounded shattered. "But it's okay."

"I'm sorry, honey," she said, sounding insincere. "Well, at least you've made a new friend."

Sometimes she treated him like he was five, not fifteen. "Mom, I know you didn't really like Sawyer, so you don't have to pretend."

"Well, they say the first heartbreak is the worst. Give it a little time and you'll be fine."

If only.

For the next hour, he lounged around in front of the TV, played a few video games, ate some chips. He didn't call Sawyer.

There was something else he had to do. Something important. Hopping on his bike, he rode over to Kevin's house. More and more, he'd come to dread these visits; the heavy smell of sickness that permeated the house, the hushed voices, and whispered conversations all added to the sense of tragedy surrounding Kevin's family.

When Francis rang the doorbell, Kevin slipped outside,

still in his pajamas. He pulled the door softly shut behind him. "This isn't a good time," he said, his voice ragged.

Francis nodded. "Tell your dad I stopped by."

Kevin's face clouded. "I can't. He fell into a coma this morning."

They stood on the doorstep awkwardly, neither boy knowing what to say to the other.

"I'm sorry." Francis wished he could find the words Kevin needed to hear. "I'll see you tomorrow, right? Call or text me if you need anything."

"Yeah," said Kevin. "If I can." His shoulders slumped. "See you around." He went back inside and shut the door.

Francis rode slowly home, his heart heavy. Kevin seemed almost zombielike, and who could blame him? When he got home, he knew he had to see his dad. He found him out in the back garden planting bulbs. For a few minutes, he stood and watched him work. Only when he thought he could control his voice did he try to speak.

"Dad…" It was no good. His voice quavered.

His dad dropped his tools immediately. "Is he gone?"

"He's in a coma."

His dad wrapped him up in a big bear hug. "I'm so sorry." He held him tightly. "But I'm glad you had the chance to say a proper good-bye."

"Bon voyage," corrected Francis, licking his dry lips. "We said bon voyage."

"Hmm."

"Mr. Croyden thought it would be better that way."

• • •

At five-thirty, Jack showed up. As soon as he walked through the front door, he whistled. "Nice digs." His eyes drank in the plush surroundings. "Seriously nice. You *are* a rich kid! Sorry, that was kind of rude, but I thought maybe Sawyer might have exaggerated. You know her."

Francis shrugged. "Yeah, whatever." He was getting tired of being labeled by these two all the time. "Follow me." He took Jack into the den, hoping he wouldn't be as impressed with the little room where the family liked to watch movies together, as he would have been with the living room. "Sit." He pointed to a tattered chair and closed the door.

But Jack didn't sit. Instead, he picked up a Scotch decanter from the mahogany sideboard and turned it over in his hands. He replaced it reverently. "Hey. Question. How did you get my cell number? You said you didn't talk to Sawyer, and I'm sure as shit I never gave it to you."

"I called your father." Francis didn't want to think about the ugly voice at the other end of the line. "He didn't want to give me your number, but I told him I was your boss and that you'd lost your wallet."

"Serious?"

"Yeah."

"I bet that was a real pleasant conversation." Jack laughed. He plunked down into the chair. "So what's up? I assume it has something to do with Sawyer."

Francis blushed. "I liked her a lot. I still do. And I'm sorry. And I don't have anyone to talk to."

"No hard feelings. Clearly you're not used to dealing with shit."

"Yeah. It might look that way, but the thing is, I've got a lot of shit going down. My best friend's dad is dying. I have an ex-girlfriend who's pregnant, and I don't know what to do. I've got Christmas exams coming up. How the hell do I tell my parents that they are going to be grandparents to a baby they'll probably never know?"

Jack covered his eyes with his hands in mock distress. "Jesus! And you thought *I* might be able to help you out?"

"Kind of. At least, I hoped you might have some ideas." He knew he didn't have the right to ask for help, but he kept his eyes steady under Jack's questioning gaze.

Finally, Jack spoke. "You've come to the right person. Let's start with Sawyer and go from there."

Chapter Eight

By the fifth month, your baby weighs about
13 ounces (360 g) and is about 10.5 inches
(27 cm) long. If you talk, read, or sing to your
baby, you can expect your infant to hear you!

Excerpt: *From Conception to Birth*

"Call her," Jack had said.

Francis had ignored his advice.

Two weeks later, on December 21, Francis and his family traded Vancouver's damp cold for Hawaii's hot sun and turquoise surf, but for the first time in memory, Francis wasn't looking forward to their annual Christmas vacation on Maui's sandy white beaches. He'd expected to feel remorse about leaving Kevin in such a bad way, but the guilt that haunted him about Sawyer and the baby and no solution came as a surprise.

After all, they'd had no contact with each other for weeks.

In truth, Jack's visit had made everything so real. It had left him cold and scared. Suddenly nothing seemed important, not Maui, not Christmas, and especially not his family. In fact, the energy it took to act like his old, carefree self drained him.

In contrast, his little brothers couldn't control their excitement at the thought of three glorious weeks on the beach. When they arrived at the airport for their early-morning flight, it took the full attention of both their parents to contain them.

Francis had no patience for their craziness. To his mom's surprise, he snapped at them, before escaping into his headphones. "Leave me alone!" he threatened, and not even Nate's tears or Devon's hurt expression softened him.

With both of them out of the way, Francis decided to send a text to Sawyer. *Have to go to Maui. Back Jan 12. Talk then?*

She shot back a reply dripping in sarcasm: *Poor U. Forced to spend 3 weeks in paradise, while we're all stuck here in the gray, cold rain.*

No mention of any baby.

Kevin dropping off Xmas gifts, he texted. He hit send. No response.

Buying her a Christmas present had been a last-minute idea, but he'd put a lot of thought into getting the perfect gift. Sawyer was easy, because he knew how much she loved to read. Although he'd spent hours poring over books, he'd been unable to settle on a title that he could be sure she hadn't read. In the end, he got her a gift certificate for her local bookstore on Main Street, along with a journal and a fountain pen, because he knew she liked to write. He hoped she'd see this for what he meant it to be—a peace offering.

His dad shook him out of his thoughts. "Wake up, Francis. It's time to board. We haven't even left the ground, and you're a million miles away."

"Sorry, Dad." He gathered his things and followed the other business-class passengers onto the plane. There were definitely perks to having a pilot for a father. With only two wide, comfy seats per row, Francis could sit alone.

But Nate had other ideas. "I want to be with Francis," he cried when he spotted the empty seat beside his big brother.

"Not a chance." Francis scowled at him. "Get lost."

Nate stuck out his tongue and scuttled back to his seat. "Meany," he called over his shoulder.

Francis pretended not to hear him, but he felt like a jerk. Too bad. He had one goal: to block out everything and everyone around him. Finding a movie, he upped the volume and sat back with his glass of orange juice and a plate of cookies—another perk of business class. Behind him, his parents sipped on champagne.

Despite all these creature comforts, he still found it hard to concentrate. His mind was racing, and he couldn't control it. Once airborne, he turned his thoughts to Kevin, picturing him and his mom in their big house. The last time he'd seen Kevin, he'd been fraught with tension. In an effort to help, Francis had the bright idea to ask him to join them in Maui. He'd come with them a few times over the years and they always had an excellent time.

"Are you serious?" Kevin had responded, his voice raising to a fevered pitch. "It's going to be our last Christmas as a family. Obviously I can't take off, and I don't want to." He tacked on, "But thanks," not meaning it.

As usual, Francis felt like a stupid jerk. What a dumb idea. "No problem. I guess I'll see you in three weeks."

As he turned to go, Kevin stopped him. "Are you okay? I mean, the Sawyer thing? You're acting kind of weird. You seem, I don't know, different."

Francis wanted to shout, *No, I'm not okay*. But instead he shrugged. "Don't worry about me."

They arrived in Maui in the early afternoon. Francis made a feeble attempt to feign some enthusiasm over their ocean-front suite, but he failed miserably. His parents didn't confront him, but his mother's quietness and his father's set lips betrayed their worry. The twins kept their distance, still angry with him for the way he'd behaved toward them earlier. "You're no fun anymore," Devon accused, and Francis couldn't deny it. Nor could he explain the confusion and anger that boiled inside of him. How could he explain the guilty relief he felt at being an ocean away from Sawyer? He felt like a coward, but he kept reminding himself that none of it was his fault, not really. *She'd screwed up. Not me.*

• • •

With the passing of each sunny day, his temper darkened. As their vacation approached its end, he began to dread returning to Canada. He both fretted that he didn't hear from Sawyer and thanked his last few lucky stars that he hadn't. Didn't she like his gift? Did she not get how much effort he'd put into finding the right things?

Finally, on January 10, she texted: *Xcellent presents. Hope U R not suffering too badly on the beach. Haha.* His mood brightened. No mention of a baby. If she really hated him, she wouldn't contact him at all—would she?

The day before their departure, Francis sought out some alone time on the beach. He loved the feel of the wet sand between his toes and the warm sun on his shoulders. The repetitive motion of the waves lulled him, so when his dad plunked down beside him, he started.

"A penny for your thoughts, son."

"I was just wishing we didn't have to leave tomorrow," Francis replied wistfully. "I wish we could stay here forever."

"You say that every year," his dad pointed out, but then his tone grew more serious. "Your mom and I can't help but notice how preoccupied you've been. At first you didn't want to be here at all. Nate and Devon are hurt. They think they've done something to anger you, but I know that's not it. Is there anything you want to talk about?"

"No, Dad." He stood up. "I just need you all to leave me alone. Is that too much to ask?" He stormed away, leaving his father stunned. Francis had lied. He wanted nothing else but to talk to his dad, but he didn't know how or where to begin.

Obviously, he couldn't solve this problem on his own, but he couldn't find the words or the courage to tell his parents the truth. If they knew what he'd done, they'd never forgive him, and why should they? He couldn't forgive himself.

Part Two

I choose to love this time for once
with all my intelligence
　　　　—Adrienne Rich (Splittings)

Chapter Nine

The baby weighed heavily on Sawyer's mind. Every time she thought about it, which was all the time, an image of what she might look like popped into her mind. Tiny, round, red-faced, wailing, smiling, gurgling, spitting…but her daydreams and thoughts were always interrupted by the same niggling ugly thought: *I'm not ready to be a mother. I'm sixteen years old.* Then the tears came, always the tears.

The wail of police sirens and red lights outside her window painted a pattern on her blank face as the emergency vehicles circled the street below her. She watched, her fists clenched and her lips pale. For a nightmarish second, she thought they might be coming for her. Then she remembered. *I'm pregnant. I'm not sick.*

She needed to talk to Francis. Didn't he have a right to know what she'd decided? Shouldn't he share this? He was as much to blame as she was. But he'd been such a jerk—except for the presents he'd given her for Christmas, she'd heard nothing from him. Not a word.

She'd been working hard to build up her strength, following the doctor's orders, taking her vitamins and iron pills religiously. She'd also made a real effort to improve her diet and get enough sleep so that she could go to school every day and concentrate on her work. The morning sickness had subsided, but she still got sick now and then. She looked forward to a vomit-free day in her near future.

Eventually, she'd broken down and told her mother about the baby. She'd thought it would be the hardest thing she'd ever done, but it wasn't. In the end, she realized she hadn't given her mother the credit she deserved.

"I'm not eating at Joe's anymore," she'd said, by way of an opener.

"I didn't know you were eating there at all," her mom scolded. "That's disgusting. It's all nachos with processed cheese and hotdogs. We're surrounded by really good fruit and veggie stores. You can get good food a stone's throw from our apartment. You know how to cook."

Francis's mother feeds her children. Why doesn't mine?

As if reading her mind, her mother said, "You're almost seventeen. Surely you can cook for yourself without pouting."

"And, I'm taking vitamins," Sawyer pressed on.

"That's good. It's time you started taking care of yourself. You know," her mom added gently, "put the past where it belongs. Our lives are here now."

"Mom…" She tried not to sound exasperated, but her mother kept changing the subject. "I'm also taking iron pills. The doctor I saw at the clinic with Jack and Francis told me I am anemic."

"You went to the clinic with Jack? What did the doctor say? Are you really sick?"

"Well, that's sort of what I'm trying to tell you, in a kind of roundabout way…" She played with a strand of hair, resisting the urge to pull it.

"What are you trying to tell me, *exactly?* No mincing words, Sawyer. Whatever it is, spit it out."

"I'm…I'm pregnant."

Her mother's face turned a sickly white. She sank like a bag of rocks onto the sofa.

"Mom! Say something," Sawyer cried. "I'm sorry."

"Oh good Christ-on-a-rope." Her mother's eyes widened and she burst into tears.

Sawyer had anticipated every reaction except this one. "Mom?" She touched her on her shoulder, but her mother pushed her hand away.

"Don't. Please, give me a few minutes."

Sawyer shoved a tissue into her mother's hand. "Here." She sat down beside her. "I'm sorry, Mom."

After a few minutes, her mother blew her nose. When she looked up, her pink, splotched face seemed years older. "I don't understand. I know Jack is gay, so how did this happen?"

"Mom, it wasn't Jack. It was Francis."

"Francis? The rich kid? He did this to you?"

"No, I mean, he didn't *do* it to me. It was consenting. I consented. It was more my idea than his."

"Oh god," her mother moaned. She stood up and paced from one end of the room to the other. "Okay, what's done is done, right? So how many months along are you? In a case like this, there's good reason to terminate. How many months?"

She'd been dreading this question. "Four months when I found out. That's not an option anymore."

"What? My god! Okay. Okay. So that's that." She stopped at the window and fiddled with the blind. Words, usually her forte, deserted her. She took a big breath. "Okay. I've got this."

"Mom, you already said that, like three times. Are you mad at me?"

"Mad at you?" She looked incredulous. "That doesn't even begin to cover what I'm thinking and feeling right now. I'm sorry this happened. I'm mad at that rich boy, but mostly we need to figure out a plan." Sitting down beside Sawyer, she gathered her into her arms. "Together."

Sawyer snuggled into her mother's soft body and, for the first time in as long as she could remember, she felt safe and loved. She could face this with her mother on her side, even if Francis was a complete jerk.

"Mom, I don't want to keep the baby. I've really thought about this. I want to graduate high school and go to university, like I planned, but I…" She paused. "I want to find the baby a good home." Her voice caught. "Can you help me?"

"It's the right thing to do," agreed her mother. "Of course I'll help you. I'll be beside you the whole way. It's the right thing to do," she repeated, "and not just for the baby, but for everyone involved…And Francis?" She practically spat out his name. "Does he have an opinion?"

"We broke up. He won't talk to me. He's jealous because he thinks Jack could be the father. Can you believe it?" She started to cry. "I guess I don't owe him anything at this point, but I want him to know the truth."

"Typical," her mother muttered under her breath. "He has a legal right to know. You have to tell him the baby is his, and he has to tell his parents. They all have a say in this, although in the end, the decision is yours and nobody else's. It's your body—you are in charge."

"Jack says he thinks fathers have rights."

"Francis is not a father. He's a kid who made a mistake. Just like you. How old is he?"

"Fifteen."

"Kids having kids. From now on, you're under my care as far as diet goes. We are going to give this baby a good start, and we're going to do that by making sure it is healthy and strong when it is born, and that we find it a really good family."

"You don't have to call it *it*."

"You know the sex?"

"It's a girl. I know it's a girl." Sawyer's tone and eyes dared her mother to argue with her.

"Okay. I'll start doing research about how to arrange for a private adoption."

• • •

That night, they shared their first meal together in months. When Jack crept in late, he sensed something different in the apartment. He couldn't quite put his finger on it, but change was in the air.

The next morning, Sawyer woke early, feeling restless. She had unfinished homework. She padded into the kitchen silently, not wanting to wake the heavily snoring Jack, whose long legs dangled over the end of the couch like those of a stick insect. Although Jack had initially intended to bunk with them for a few days, both Sawyer and her mom had agreed that he should stay until he found something more permanent. He'd been reluctant at first, but they'd expected that. Jack never wanted to be a bother. That was part of his charm.

She found a box of oatmeal and a banana on the table, beside a note from her mother. *Eat up. This is good for you. Full of potassium, fiber, and lots of other vitamins and minerals. I love you! Mom.*

Sawyer tucked the note into her pocket. She couldn't remember the last time her mother had said that. Still, she opted to skip breakfast, deciding to grab tea and a muffin on the way to school. Wiggling into her leggings, she noticed they were a bit tight around the middle. *Great!* She grabbed her backpack and slipped out the door into the gray light of dawn.

Hungry, she entered the first diner she came across. It was a bit shabby, but it would have to do. Except for an elderly woman, it was empty, and despite its claim of *Homemade Food, Cheap and Delicious*, it didn't smell delicious. Behind the laminate counter, a middle-aged man in a stained apron waved his fat fingers and greeted her with a friendly "Hello. Coffee?"

"Tea, please." Sawyer sat down on a stool at the counter.

"Tea," the man shouted toward the kitchen.

In no time, a small woman shuffled out of the kitchen and placed a mug of steaming water and a tea bag in front of Sawyer. "Something to eat?" she asked.

"Whole wheat toast and strawberry jam, please," she said, shrinking under the woman's intense stare.

Her catlike eyes shone. "You know, I read fortunes. Says so right on the door. Maybe I can read yours."

"I don't have any money," Sawyer said, interested.

The woman cackled and sat down beside her. "It won't take a minute, and I'll do it free of charge."

She snatched Sawyer's hand and ran her dry, wrinkled fingers over her palm. "Let's see," she murmured. "You're troubled. I see two boys in your present and a man in your past…and there are two other males…and…my goodness! You've got a baby girl! That's what is getting you down. She's fine, though."

Sawyer quickly withdrew her hand. "Oh my god, I knew it. But how did you?" She looked down at her tummy.

The old woman retrieved her hand and shushed her. "There's more. Who is London?"

"London? London isn't a person. It's the place I come from—where I used to live."

"No," the woman replied with finality. "That's not what I'm seeing at all." She dropped Sawyer's hand onto the counter. "Saying good-bye to London won't be easy, but it's the right thing to do."

Chapter Ten

Sawyer met Jack outside the coffee shop so they could walk home together. On the way, Jack listened attentively while Sawyer described the greasy diner. "It's called the Purple Onion. Dumb name," she scoffed. "And you should have seen the way they looked at me when I walked in, as if they were expecting me." She frowned. "At first I thought the lady was crazy when she insisted on reading my palm, but she knew stuff about me, stuff impossible to guess."

"I don't know," Jack disagreed. "Maybe your pregnancy was just a lucky guess. And, after all, it's fifty-fifty whether it will be a girl or a boy. It doesn't seem like rocket science to me."

"What about the London part? Doesn't that seem a bit on the hocus-pocus side to you?"

"Yeah. That part's a bit weird. But what did she mean by the two boys, the man in your past, and the mysterious males in your life?"

"That's easy," said Sawyer. "You and Francis are the two boys, and my dad is obviously the man. As for the others, I think she got that part wrong."

"Yeah." Jack flicked his hair out of his eyes. "Personally, I think it's all a load of crap."

Sawyer elbowed Jack playfully. "It wouldn't hurt you to believe in a little magic once in a while."

"Give me a reason to," Jack replied.

Sawyer sighed and changed the subject. "Sometimes I hear a baby crying." She looked at him with scared eyes. "Do you think it's because I'm pregnant? Do you think the baby is mad at me because I'm not going to keep her?"

Jack stopped in the middle of the sidewalk and placed his hands on Sawyer's shoulders. "Now, you listen to me. I don't know much about having a baby, except that it involves a lot of barfing and not much sleep. But one thing I do know for sure is that you are doing the right thing for yours." Jack spoke with an authority he did not feel. He walked away, his head down.

Sawyer caught up with him and cast him a knowing glance. "Know what? I do understand how important it is."

Reminding himself that he could trust this girl more than anyone in the world, he took a deep breath. "I haven't had a lot of luck in life. It's taken a huge effort for me to be a good person…" He threw her a self-deprecating smile. "And as stupid as it sounds, I've wished my mother had found me a good home, before she left me with him."

"Oh, Jack. I'm sorry." She took his hand and squeezed it. "You do have a home and a family. You have us. And thank you…You always know what to say when I doubt myself." She sidled up to him. "I wish you were straight," she teased, and was delighted to hear his laughter.

They continued walking until they got to Sawyer's house. As she extracted her keys from her bag, she gave him a hug. "I mean it. Thanks. You are a true friend. And you know, as far as barfing goes, the morning sickness is pretty much gone. In fact, I've got my appetite back, and now I'm starving all the time." She unlocked the door and they climbed the stairs. Inside the upstairs apartment, they made a beeline for the kitchen. "And another thing you should know," Sawyer confided. "I told my mom about the baby."

"Whoa! That's huge! What did she say?"

"You'll crack up. She wanted to know how it happened, you being gay and all."

"What? *She* thought it was me?" Jack sputtered.

"Not for long. I told her it was Francis. She doesn't like him. She calls him the rich kid, like it's a curse or something."

"He is a rich kid, but he's a good kid too," Jack replied, to Sawyer's surprise.

"Wow, that's the first time you've said anything positive about him. Mom says I have to talk to him, but he's so mad at me, me and you. Still, he left me a book, journal, and pen, you know, and I blew it off."

"Would you kill me if I told you I've talked to him?"

Her eyes narrowed. "Yes. I'd double-kill you."

"Fine. I won't tell you, then." He opened the fridge. "Who stocked up on all the healthy food?" He rifled around until he found an apple and a lemon square.

"Don't try to change the subject, Jack. Come on. Spill it. Did you see Francis? Where? When? What did he say? Did he call you?"

"Not exactly. Here." He offered her a glass of apple juice, but she pushed it away.

"Tell me you didn't call him. I'll kill you if you did."

"I did." He splayed his arms to each side, like Jesus on the cross. "Slay me."

Sawyer punched him lightly in the stomach. "Spit it out. Right now."

"I did it because if it weren't for me pawing you and talking about sleeping overnight, you two might still be together. It was my fault you broke up, so I figured it was up to me to get you back together. There's my motive, but stranger than strange, I think Francis and I will be friends. And," he added quickly, "I told him why the baby couldn't be mine."

He held his breath, prepared for her fury. He knew she preferred to fight her own battles, but she just nodded.

"It's okay, Jack. Someone had to tell him, and I figured your sexuality is yours to disclose. Or not. What did he say?"

"He wanted to kill me. I think he really hoped I was the father."

"Holy shit. What is it about the word *gay* that people don't get? And what happened when you explained your sexual orientation?"

"I gotta be honest with you. He's more cool with the gay thing than with the idea of being a dad."

"He's not going to be a dad, Jack. He's the sperm donor.

Nothing more. Is there anything else you haven't told me?"

Jack looked at his watch. "Um, yeah. Francis will be here in about six minutes. And before you lambaste me, know that I did it for you. You shouldn't have to go through this baby thing alone."

"I'm not alone," Sawyer protested. "I've got you and my mom. I thought I loved Francis, but now I'm not so sure. We are from such different worlds. Maybe I'm too young to be in love."

"You know, you don't have to love Francis to let him be a part of this. And your worlds aren't as far apart as you think. He's a kid, with kid issues, like us."

Before she could reply, there was a tentative rap on the door. "Oh my god. It's him." She looked at Jack, her eyes wild.

"So, let him in."

"It's open!" she yelled in the general direction of the door.

Francis poked his head into the room. He looked so terrified that Jack felt sorry for him. "Hey, Francis. Come on in."

He stepped warily into the room. "Hi, Sawyer. Jack." He stood half in, half out the doorway, unsure of what to say, how to behave, or where to look.

Jack breezed past him. "Actually, I'm on my way out."

Sawyer thought differently. "You can't leave."

"I have a shift." He placed his hands firmly on her shoulders and moved her out of his way. "I'll see you later," he promised, bolting out the door.

After Jack's hurried departure, it took a few long seconds for Francis to dig up the courage to speak. "So, I talked to Jack. About…you know…I know he's…you know…"

"Gay?" Sawyer finished the sentence for him. "Yup. Old news around here."

"So, I'm the...well, you're not...you don't look pregnant yet."

She turned to show him her profile and pulled her T-shirt snug against her body. "It's pretty obvious."

Francis saw a barely discernible bump—it didn't look like a baby at all. "You look like you swallowed a tiny cantaloupe. I thought you'd be huge."

"Thanks. That's exactly the right thing to say." Sawyer snorted.

He took a step closer. "No. I mean you look good. Jack said you'd been feeling better. Not sick anymore?"

"I'm pretty much over the morning sickness now."

"Oh." Francis shifted uncertainly from foot to foot. He knew nothing about having a baby and looked at Sawyer helplessly. "Oh."

"Yeah. My mom says she puked for most of the nine months she carried me."

Francis thought he might throw up on his shoes. "Your mom? Your mom knows? How...? You didn't tell her about... well, you know, about...?"

"About you? Of course I did."

"Is your mom pissed at me?"

"She's okay. At first she suspected Jack. Just like you did," she teased, clearly enjoying his discomfort.

"Well, how was I supposed to know?" He grinned, feeling like an idiot. "I'm sorry for what I said."

"I don't know if I'm ready to forgive you, but I'll try," Sawyer conceded.

Francis forced himself to raise his eyes to meet hers. "There are options, you know. I looked it up online."

Her eyes narrowed. "Wrong. There *were* options a couple of months ago, but those options are gone now. You can't have an abortion after three months. It's the law. Besides, you think it's easy to make that kind of a decision?"

He didn't bother to disguise his disappointment. "So, you're having it?"

"Her. And yes. I'm having her, Francis."

"Or him."

"No. It's been confirmed. The baby's a her. I had my palm read."

"Very scientific," he scorned. "And then what?"

"Don't worry. I've put a lot of thought into this, and I'm going to find a good family for her. Mom said she'd help me. Jack's in too."

"And what about me? Where do I fit in?"

He flinched under her scathing glare. "Wow! Like it's any of your business. Like you care about her or me. Jesus, Francis. You won't talk to me on the phone. You don't answer my texts. You're only here because Jack made you come, and even then, you've taken your time. None of this is any of your affair, not anymore." She hadn't meant to lose her temper, but he infuriated her.

For his part, Francis had never felt so ashamed. "I'm sorry," he repeated.

"I thought," she continued, "that I loved you, but maybe I don't. Maybe I actually hate you. I didn't want you to come here, but when Jack said he'd contacted you, I figured you felt bad, but you don't feel anything at all." Although she spoke calmly, he could see the effort it cost her.

"Sawyer, what am I supposed to tell my parents?" He buried his face in his hands.

"So *that's* what's bugging you?" Her face reddened, and she swiped her nose with her sleeve. "But since you asked, you could try the truth."

The truth. The truth was, he didn't want a baby. The truth was, it was too late now. He couldn't wish it away. The truth was, he was terrified to talk to his parents. "Okay. But on one condition. Let me help you and your mom and Jack find the right home. For her."

Sawyer regarded him steadily. There didn't seem a whole lot more to say, so she simply nodded. Francis bit his top lip and waited for her to speak first. Finally, she broke the silence. "How is Kevin's dad?"

"Mr. Croyden? He's in a coma. He's dying."

"I'm sorry," she said, meaning it. "Francis, I want my baby to have good parents. A father that sticks around for a while."

"Kevin's dad isn't exactly choosing to cut out," Francis said.

"Sorry." Sawyer said quietly. "Point taken."

Francis nodded. "I know what you're saying. A dad who isn't abusive, like Jack's."

Chapter Eleven

Kevin had to get out of the house. He grabbed his jacket, scribbled a short, evasive note to his mom saying he'd be back in a few hours, then hopped an east-bound bus. He doubted his mother would read it or even see it. She hadn't left his dad's side since he'd fallen into the coma. Kevin had to leave. He couldn't bear another second of watching his father fade away. Francis had texted him that he'd be at Sawyer's and that Kevin could follow him there if he needed to get away. He remembered where she lived, more or less, and if he couldn't find her house, so be it. At least he'd be distracted for a few hours.

He got off the bus near 13th and Main and wandered aimlessly for almost an hour. Secondhand shops battled cafés and funky clothing stores for sidewalk space. In a different mood and on a drier day, he would have liked to do some exploring.

He was thinking about returning home when he spotted

Jack. The gay kid. He'd seen him talking to Francis at school
the other day. Emo looking guy. Street smart. Nice, though.

"Hey," he called out. "Jack!"

Jack looked up, startled. "Kevin?"

"I'm looking for Francis."

Jack eyed him. The guy didn't look well. Dark circles surrounded his eyes. He was even skinnier than before. "Francis is
with Sawyer. They need some alone time. I don't think they'd
be thrilled to see you."

Jack had lied when he told Sawyer and Francis he had
to work. When Kevin ran into him, he'd just planted himself
under a daffodil-colored awning and lit up a smoke, wondering
where he could hang for the next hour. He drew deeply on the
cigarette now and considered the situation. The acrid smoke
filled his lungs, and he relaxed as the nicotine cruised through
his bloodstream. He'd have to quit soon. At eleven bucks a
pack, he didn't have much choice, but he hated to give up this
one indulgence.

The brooding sky matched Jack's mood. *Damn rain!* He
pulled up his jacket collar and butted out his cigarette. "You
can hang out with me if you want."

"Sure," Kevin agreed, desperate. "Anything but home."

Main Street, normally choked with traffic, was deserted. *It
was a good day to be at home.* As grateful as Jack was for Sawyer's
couch and her mother's generosity, he knew he couldn't crash
there forever. Eventually he'd have to find a place of his own.
That meant he'd need more money, so more shifts at work. He
sighed, thinking that his schoolwork would suffer.

The boys cruised along the street in silence, each preoccupied with his own problems. Kevin tried to remember his dad before the cancer. *Life isn't fair.* Secretly, he hoped for a miracle. He'd read about lots of sick people who got better and not even the doctors could explain it. He wasn't terribly religious, but he prayed all the time. *I know you don't know me, God, but if you exist, here's your chance to prove it.*

While Kevin implored a god for an intervention, Jack thought about Francis's life. He had it all. A big fancy house, a posh private school, devoted parents, and sweet brothers, according to Sawyer. He wouldn't have minded being adopted into *that* family.

On top of everything else, Francis had a father who loved him. *Life isn't exactly fair.*

Lost in thought, Jack realized they'd ended up at the foot of the narrow cul-de-sac, outside the dumpy bungalow he had called home for the last five years. He stepped back into the shadow of the trees. *I should get out of here.* He'd been only thirteen when his dad moved them into the dank basement suite. Granted, it was a big improvement over the hotel room they'd lived in before, or the one before that. In this place, he'd been able to stand up straight, for a few years, anyway. However, by fifteen, he had to either duck or risk whacking his head on the exposed pipes that snaked over the low, water-stained ceiling.

"Where are we?" Kevin asked nervously, sensing Jack's anxiety.

On the spot, Jack made up his mind. "Kevin, you're about to see how bad it can get when you're not born into a *nice* family."

Jack spotted his dad's only pride and joy, a battered Chevy truck, rusting in the driveway and waiting for a windfall that would never come to pay for insurance. Its cracked windshield and flaking paint spoke of better days when his dad had worked steadily—days long gone. Welfare covered beer, smokes, rent, the sports channel, and food, in that order. Jack conjured up an image of his dad crashed on the couch doing what he did best—chugging a beer and watching a football game. Jack lit another cigarette to keep his anger in check, offering one to Kevin, who shook his head. "Nah. I've seen up close."

When he'd smoked it down to the filter, Jack crunched the cigarette beneath the heel of his boot, his mind made up. "Follow me, and keep quiet."

Kevin hesitated briefly, then, crouching low like Jack, he moved stealthily around the side of the neglected old truck and over the uneven path that snaked around the side of the house. Staying close on Jack's heels, he took care not to catch his school jacket on the jagged stucco wall. They stopped beside a dirty window. Jack held his fingers to his lips and pointed. Kevin peeked through the grimy pane, where he saw a heavy, unshaven man sprawled on a grease-stained couch, like a beached whale.

"My dad," Jack hissed. "He was so proud of that stupid sofa when he scored it out of a back alley. Filthy piece of crap."

"That's your father?" whispered Kevin. "Are you sure you want to go in there?"

Jack nodded. In spite of everything, he resented his kicked-out status. "You wouldn't understand. You stay here. I'll call you if

I need you." He was tired of depending on the kindness of other people for his survival. His fingers went unconsciously to the pocket in his jeans where he had kept the house key ever since his father had told him to take his "sorry pansy ass" elsewhere.

Jack slunk away. Kevin kept his eyes on the body on the couch. If it weren't for the can of beer moving up and down rhythmically to his mouth, he would have thought him dead. The floor beside him was strewn with empties and a half-empty bag of potato chips.

While Kevin waited nervously, Jack made his way to the backyard and down three mossy concrete steps to the rotting door. He wiggled the key into the rusty lock and crept silently into the tiny hall, confident his dad wouldn't hear him over the sound of the massive 52-inch TV that dwarfed everything else in the cramped room.

"To hell with it," he muttered to himself, taking a step into the living room. He forgot to duck and banged his head hard on an exposed pipe. "Shit!" he exploded, followed by a more contrite, "Hi, Dad."

His father didn't seem at all surprised to see him. "How many goddamned times do I have to tell you about that pipe until you get it through your thick skull?" He spoke with contempt, never dragging his eyes from the TV screen. "What the fuck do you want?" He burped.

Jack's resolve disappeared, along with any hope of moving back in. "I thought I'd drop in. See what's up."

"Football. It's always football in the afternoons. You know that." He took a swig of beer.

"Who's winning?"

"Like you even know who's playing, you dumb shit."

Jack stood rooted to the ground. This had been a monumental mistake, but his father hadn't finished insulting him yet. "Football isn't a fag's game, Jacky."

"I have plenty of friends who like football."

"You mean footsie, don't you?" His father laughed at his own joke, spraying beer over his chest.

"I want to come back home," Jack blurted. That's not what he had meant to say. The words spewed out all on their own, like vomit. What he'd meant to say was "Go to hell."

"I want to come home," his dad simpered. "Are you still a queer, 'cause if you are, no queers allowed under my roof." He snorted at his own words. "Did you take an anti-queer course, like I told you to?"

"Dad," Jack said helplessly. "I told you. It's not like that. I don't have a choice."

"Fuck you. You don't have a choice." For a big man, he moved like lightning. The beer can hit Jack square above his right eye. He fell to his knees, temporarily blinded by the blood pouring down his face.

Shit! Kevin thought, too scared to move or to be heard. He could see and hear everything through the cracked windowpane.

"You asshole!" Jack screamed.

His dad's lip curled. "It's just a tiny cut. Stop whimpering and stand on your feet like a man," he sneered. "Although I guess you like being on your knees." He laughed again, louder and meaner this time, enjoying himself.

Jack scrambled to his feet and ran to the bathroom, not wanting his father or Kevin to see him cry. He splashed cold water on his face and pressed a wad of toilet paper against the cut to stop the bleeding. The cut would leave a nice little scar over his right eye to match the nice little scar on his left brow; he'd be reminded of his dad every time he looked in a mirror. He kicked the wall. He didn't know who he hated more, his father for being such a bully or his mother for leaving him in his care. Sawyer had options. Surely his mom had had options too. Why did she leave him behind? She could have found a nice family for him…Why had she left him with a mean drunk who hated him?

Even their coloring differed. It comforted Jack to know that he took after his mother. Like her, he was tall with an angular face and had enormous blue eyes that turned heads. He must have inherited her long fingers—the fingers of a piano player—because his dad's hands were stubby. He loved the idea of his mother, but he'd never understand why she'd chosen this brute of a man, with his mean piggy eyes the color of mud and his round, jowly face. Even from this far away, Jack's nose crinkled at the stink of beer, sweat, and misery.

Jack booted open the bathroom door. On his way out, he punched a hole in the drywall. His dad sat up, following Jack's every move. "I'm done," Jack hollered. "If you ever touch me again, or come near me again, I'll kill you."

Jack expected he'd have to defend himself, but his dad sank down onto the couch, his mouth gaping. "You sound just like your mother did before she took off."

"Who could blame her? I just wish she'd taken me."

"Ha. She would have, but I put my foot down. It killed her to leave you, but she figured I'd kill her if she took you."

Jack calmly straightened his jacket and stepped on each empty beer can, crushing them beneath the heel of his boot. Not once did he take his eyes off his father's face. When he'd annihilated them all, his upper lip curled into a snarl. "You've just given me the only thing I ever needed from you, and for that one and only thing, I thank you. My mom didn't leave me because she wanted to. She did it because you gave her no choice. Fuck you!" he said, walking out the door for the last time.

Jack rounded the corner, almost tripping over Kevin. "Get up," he ordered. "Let's get out of here."

Kevin scrambled to his feet. "That prick," he said. "I didn't know if I should call the cops." He looked at Jack with admiration. "You were awesome!"

In the driveway, Jack smashed the side mirror on the truck. He wrenched the windshield wipers off and chucked them into the bushes. Kevin watched, but he didn't try to stop him. When he'd done all the damage his rage allowed for, Kevin took Jack's arm and led him away. They headed back to Main Street.

"Feeling better?" Kevin asked after a while.

Jack smiled. "Oh yeah!"

"You're not planning on going back there again, are you?"

"Nope." He seemed strangely happy. "I've got a plan. I'm going to try to get more shifts at work, maybe ask for a raise."

Kevin had never met anyone quite like Jack. "Does your boss like you?"

"Yeah. I'm good at my job."

"You seem good at a lot of things. So you deserve it. Go for it."

"Thanks, Kevin." Jack stopped. "I mean it. Thanks for having my back."

"I didn't do anything."

Jack smiled. "I know. But you would have. And I'm sorry about your dad. I really am. Francis says he is one of the good guys. Not like my old man."

Kevin nodded. "I'm lucky. It's hard to lose him, but I'm damn lucky. Thanks for making me see that."

"You are lucky," Jack agreed. "I would give anything to have a dad who loved me. Don't forget it." He patted Kevin on the back.

Kevin looked at his watch. "I have to go. I've got a soccer game in a couple of hours."

"Hope you win."

"Thanks." Kevin grinned. "And you might want to remove the toilet paper from your forehead."

"Yup. Good idea. I'll see you around." Jack felt immensely better. Now he knew his mother had wanted to take him with her when she fled. He decided to drop into the café right away, while his spirits were high. When his boss saw him, she said in alarm, "What happened to you?"

"It's a long story." When he finished talking, an hour had passed.

She couldn't hide her admiration for him or her anger. "You need to press charges against him."

"No. The best revenge is living well, and that's my plan. I'm not going to simply survive. I'm going to continue to ace school, I'm going to work hard, and I'm not looking back."

"At least let me clean up your eye." After she finished, she offered him a three-dollar hourly raise, with a promise of another dollar an hour in the summer, as well as a promotion to assistant manager. "I'm so glad you trusted me," she told him. "That took a lot of courage." She paused, then, making up her mind, added, "Jack, the guy upstairs is leaving in four months. I know it seems like a long time, but if you can wait, I'd be happy to rent that little studio apartment to you for a really reasonable price. You're underage, so we'd have to get a social worker involved, and it might be a hassle, but…?"

Jack blinked. "Yes. Yes!" To his boss's surprise, he threw his arms around her. "Thank you."

• • •

By the time he arrived at Sawyer's, Francis had left. "How'd it go?" he asked her.

Sawyer stared at him. "You look like shit. What happened to you?"

"My dad happened, for the last time. But it's okay. It's good. I don't want to talk about me. Not now. How did it go between you and Francis?"

She wouldn't get anywhere questioning him in his current mood. "It was okay." Sawyer bit into her second blueberry muffin. "We agreed on a few things—like maybe we are not in

love, and I'm going to let him help us find the baby a home."
She knitted her brows. "He hasn't told his parents about the
baby yet."

Jack smiled, then he winced because it hurt to move his
face. "Francis needs to grow up. It's not an easy thing to do, but
trust me, if he stops acting like a little kid, they'll stop treating
him like one."

Sawyer cocked her head. "You seem different, Jack. I don't
know why, but you do."

Jack grinned despite the discomfort.

Chapter Twelve

As soon as Francis left Sawyer's apartment, he sent a text to Jack: *Thx 4 keeping me in the loop. I'll do the same. Sawyer and I r officially broken up—all good. I'll help find parents 4 baby. Got some other stuff to do first.*

While he waited for the bus, Francis thought about Sawyer's parting words to him: *As cliché as it sounds, I want to be your friend, so hurry up and tell your parents about the baby. That's all you have to do to prove to me you're in this with me.* So, it was to be a group effort—Jack, Sawyer, her mom, and Francis. It seemed weird, but Sawyer always did things her way. It was one of the things Francis liked best about her.

Francis went straight from Sawyer's place to his soccer game. En route, he called Kevin. When his friend answered, he dove into the events of the afternoon. "Sawyer is having the baby. It's confirmed. I'm the dad. It's all fucked up, and I don't know what to do."

Kevin reacted just as Francis knew he would. "You've got to be fucking kidding me!"

If only.

"So, she's decided to keep the kid?"

"It's too late for her to have an abortion."

Kevin's voice lowered. "That's good."

Francis was surprised. "Are you kidding? That would have solved everything. She's not exactly old enough to be a mother."

After that, the line went kind of quiet. Francis defended himself. "If she'd had an abortion, I wouldn't have to face my parents with this."

Kevin sighed. "Does it always have to be about you?"

Francis thought this was unfair, considering how much time he'd been spending with Kevin lately. But he let it go. Kevin had bigger things to deal with.

"Yeah, well, I'll see you at the game."

"Yeah. I gotta go. My mom's calling."

"Later." They disconnected and Francis went back to thinking about his promise to Sawyer. He'd tell his parents. But how? Deciding he'd talk it over with Kevin on their walk home after the game, he hoofed it, not wanting to be late again or Coach would take another piece out of him. Kevin wasn't there when he arrived at the field, hot and sweaty, but on time. Francis cleated up, joining in the banter with the rest of the team, but only halfheartedly, as they went through their pre-game warm-up.

A couple of the boys teased him about Sawyer. "Hey, how's the girlfriend? Haven't seen much of you lately. You been doing the dirty with that Eastside chick?"

Word got around. Francis ignored them. He needed to focus on the game against Division Five—a tough and talented team they'd lost more than one game to over the season.

"Where's Croyden?" everyone wanted to know.

"I'll text him," Francis said. He texted. *Where R U? You're going to miss the game.*

Coach caught him texting and glared at him. "Okay, boys. Phones in bags. Minds on the game. We can beat these guys. Francis, where's Kevin?"

"I'm trying to reach him," Francis explained. "That's why I had my phone out."

"Okay." Coach gritted his teeth. "Not your problem. He's pulled a no-show. That means each one of you will have to put in a little more time on the field." Not showing up for a game, and not letting anyone know, broke one of the cardinal rules of play and let down the whole team. Coach looked pissed. Unless he had a damn good excuse, Kevin would be in for it at school tomorrow.

But despite being down one player, they won by a goal, and Coach suggested pizza to celebrate. Francis declined. "There's something I have to do tonight."

At home, he stripped off his outer muddy clothes in the front hall, thinking about texting Kevin again. But why should he always be the one to make first contact? *Screw it*, he decided. Upstairs, the twins swished and shrieked in the tub, ignoring their dad's half-serious laments: "Hey, keep the water in the tub! Which one of you can hold your breath the longest?" Francis smiled, glad to have his dad home for a few days.

He followed his mother's voice down the long hallway to the den. Even in the semidarkness, he could tell she'd been crying. "Mom? What's wrong?"

"Come and sit down, honey. We need to talk." She patted the cushion beside her.

Francis took a deep breath. He'd dreaded this moment and now it was here, and much worse than he'd imagined. Trying to ignore the sick feeling in his gut, he took a seat beside her.

"Francis," she whispered, "I'm so sorry."

"No, Mom. I should be the one apologizing."

She put her arm around him. "It's not your fault. How could you think that? These things happen, and they are out of our control."

"No, it's not that easy. Someone has to take the blame. That someone is me. At least fifty percent of this is my fault."

"Aw, honey. You're in no way responsible for any of this."

"Mom," Francis ventured, "what are we talking about?"

She dabbed her red-rimmed eyes with a tissue. "Kevin's father died this afternoon."

"Kevin's father died this afternoon," he repeated numbly. "But I talked to Kevin before the game and I texted him, but he didn't answer…" His voice trailed off. "Why didn't he tell me?" Francis hadn't given him a chance. He'd blurted out all of his own problems and hadn't bothered to ask Kevin a single question.

His mom sniffled. "I spoke to his mother. Poor Kevin is taking it pretty hard. And I know this isn't easy for you either. Austin was a fine man."

Choking back tears, Francis ran for the privacy of his bedroom. He was angry with himself for being so self-absorbed, but relieved he could put off telling his parents about the baby for a little longer. When his mother tapped on his door, he shouted, "Leave me alone. Please." He listened to her heavy footsteps retreating down the hall, grateful that she hadn't persisted.

• • •

He didn't wake up in time for school the next day and his parents allowed him to sleep in. When he finally appeared midmorning in the kitchen, bleary-eyed and worn out, his mother suggested they pay a visit to Kevin and his family. "I don't know what I'm supposed to say to him," Francis protested feebly.

"You don't have to say anything," his father said. "The fact that you're there will be enough. Besides, we won't stay long."

Kevin's house was crowded with close friends, cousins, aunts, and uncles. Kevin barely glanced at the sympathy card Francis offered, tossing it onto the growing pile of similar ones on the hall table. He led Francis to the back porch, complaining. "Every room in the house is filled to capacity with people."

"Look, Kevin," Francis said. "I should have asked about your dad when I called you. You were right. It shouldn't always be about me."

But Kevin didn't want to talk about his dad; instead, he wanted to know if Francis had talked to his parents.

Francis shook his head.

"Look, I'd rather talk about your problems than my own

right now. It distracts me. Nobody knows what to say to me, but I'm still me. I'm just me without Dad." His voice cracked. Francis realized the effort it took for his friend to maintain his composure. "Humor me. What were you going to say?"

"Sure. Okay. If that's what you need."

"I can't believe she's keeping the baby," Kevin whispered.

"She's going to find it a good home. And I'm not supposed to call it *it* because it's a her."

"Holy crap! That makes it so real!"

"I know. I'm going to tell them as soon as we leave here."

"Better you than me." Their conversation ended abruptly, cut short when Kevin's aunt swept onto the porch and smothered Kevin in her arms. Francis watched with empathy before he slipped away to look for his parents. He found them chatting to Kevin's uncle, looking as uncomfortable as he felt. "Ready to go?"

They walked home through the park, his mom and dad arm in arm, lost in their own thoughts. Although the cloud cover of the last few days still lingered, a sliver of sunlight managed to break through.

It was his mom who broke the silence. "They've chosen St. Andrew's Church for the service because Austin had such a big family and so many friends," his mother said sadly. "Kevin's lucky to have you, Francis, and he really needs your support right now."

Francis felt a drop of rain and then another and another. "Mom. Dad. There's something you need to know." They both stopped and stared at him, alarmed by the tone of his voice and oblivious to the raindrops. Francis plunged ahead. "I'm so ashamed and embarrassed. I assumed she wouldn't keep the baby. I thought she'd have an abortion. I'm so sorry. It wasn't supposed to turn out this way."

"Francis." Although the color had drained from his father's face, he spoke calmly. "Gather your thoughts and say what you have to say in a way that we can both understand."

His mother had understood, though. "You can't be saying what I think you are! You're too young. You're just a boy!" Her voice rose with every word. "Francis, I don't want to hear this!"

"I'm sorry," he repeated helplessly. "Everything's messed up."

"Let him talk," his father ordered in his best pilot's voice. "Give him a chance to explain himself. Go ahead, son. We won't interrupt." He shot his wife a stern look. "Will we?"

She shook her head. "But I'd like to sit down."

"No." Francis pulled away. "It's easier for me if we are walking."

Telling his parents about the baby was the hardest thing he'd ever done. They listened in shock, and when he'd finished speaking, they both stared at him blankly.

It was his father who spoke first. "Poor Sawyer. She's a brave young woman. And, Francis, I'm proud of you for having the courage to tell us the truth. Everybody makes mistakes, but not everybody handles them with such integrity."

His mother was less understanding. "Oh my god, Francis. I can't handle this right now." She quickened her pace and hurried ahead of them, her small body bent against the rain.

"I don't think she's taking this quite as well as you, Dad. I don't think she'll ever forgive me."

"Don't worry, Francis." He put his arm around Francis's shoulder and squeezed. "Your mother will come around. She loves you. We both do."

He pulled Francis closer into a hug. For the first time in memory, Francis didn't protest. "Is Sawyer one hundred percent sure she wants to place her baby up for adoption?"

Francis nodded. "It's too late for an abortion and school is really important to her. This is what she wants to do. She wants to give the baby a chance at a good life."

"Like I said, she's a brave girl. Francis, you know how much we love Nate and Devon and what a gift they are to us, don't you?"

"Yes."

"Sawyer's baby will be a blessing to a family, like your brothers were, and always will be, to us. Her decision is the right one. We need to offer her all of the support we can."

Chapter Thirteen

In the sixth month, your baby weighs nearly
1.5 pounds (660g) and measures about 14
inches (35cm). Your baby can suck her thumb
and you may feel her hiccup. Your baby's
patterns of sleep and waking are developing.

Excerpt: *From Conception to Birth*

The days leading up to Mr. Croyden's funeral were difficult
ones for Francis and for his parents. Even Devon and Nate
sensed the aura of unhappiness that hung over everyone like
a dark cloud. They showed their unease with tantrums and
bickering and managed to get on everyone's, including Ralph's,
nerves.

Yet, despite the huge emotional upheaval in the household, Francis's dad had been correct. As predicted, his mother

began to slowly accept the inevitable: Francis had made a mistake, and now they all must do their best to help find the baby a loving family—except that, to Francis's horror, she wanted to keep the baby. "We can't send the baby to strangers. After all, we're blood. We're the grandparents. The child can live with us."

"What? Are you out of your mind, Mom?"

"Enough, Francis," his dad cautioned. "Let me handle this. Honey, are you thinking we might raise the baby in our house and pretend that Francis isn't the father?" His dad's voice was heavy with concern. "You know that's impossible."

"The baby would have everything. A big family, love, a good life…" Her voice dropped off into a sob. "I know you're right, but…"

Francis slumped into the nearest chair. He hadn't expected this. He didn't want the baby. He didn't want any part of it. What was wrong with his mother? He flashed her a look of pure resentment. In turn, his father placed his finger on his lips and shook his head. *Just keep quiet.*

He folded his wife into his arms, rubbing her back gently until her shoulders stopped shaking and her cries subsided. "I know it's hard," he soothed. "But we're going to make sure this baby goes to a fantastic home. A home every bit as wonderful as the one you made for all of us."

Disgusted with himself for all the heartache he'd caused, Francis left the room, his head hung in shame.

All week, he avoided his mother, afraid that she'd want to talk to him about adopting the baby, but she didn't broach the subject again. Still, her brave face didn't fool Francis. He knew she was suffering inside and he hated himself for it. He prayed that she'd forgive him one day.

• • •

The day of the funeral dawned fair and warm, defying the cheerless hours that lay ahead. Francis woke early and lay in bed, listening to the twins' banter. He envied them for their bright moods, for their innocence. He felt fifteen going on a hundred. He'd never been to a funeral before, unless you counted the time they'd buried Tabitha, their first cat, in the back garden.

His mother tapped on his bedroom door. "Time to get ready, Francis," she called softly. "Breakfast is on the table. We'll leave in an hour."

He dressed in his school uniform, checking his face for stubble in the bathroom mirror. He'd started shaving a couple of months ago, not because he needed to, but because Kevin had assured him that if he shaved, his facial hair would grow in. So far that theory had proven incorrect.

While he inspected himself, his thoughts turned to Sawyer and Jack. He hadn't seen either of them all week, but he'd texted them both on the day Mr. Croyden passed away. A day later, he texted Sawyer again. *I've told my parents.*

Thx, she replied. *I'll text Kevin.*

Kevin had been grateful and relieved that Francis and Sawyer were talking again. "I know you and Sawyer have had your differences," he'd told Francis, "but I really like her."

"She feels the same way about you," he'd replied.

His dad bellowed to him from downstairs, interrupting his thoughts. "Francis, get a move on."

Breakfast was a dreary affair. Nate and Devon, angry that they were to be left out of things for the day, squabbled. Finally, to everyone's relief, the babysitter arrived and, under strict instruction to tire them out, she hustled them off to kindergarten with a promise that if they behaved, they would go to the park afterward. Fifteen minutes later, Francis and his parents climbed wordlessly into the car, each lost in their own thoughts. Francis sat in the back, wedged uncomfortably between the twins' car seats, which nobody had thought to remove. In the front, his mom clutched her husband's hand, her small hand invisible in his much larger one. She wore a blue dress and a short jacket in a lighter shade of cobalt, with a pale yellow scarf. His dad was equally striking in a black pinstripe suit and a crisp white shirt. "Aren't you supposed to wear black to a funeral?" Francis queried his mother.

"There are no rules anymore," she replied. "I'm wearing hopeful colors, garden colors, because I know that Austin would appreciate that." She opened her purse and handed Francis some tissues. "Put these in your pocket, just in case."

Close to two hundred people milled around outside St. Andrew's Church when they arrived, including Francis's headmaster, Coach, Mr. Haywood Smith, and all of the boys in the two grade tens at Hudson. Everyone stood in small clusters, speaking in hushed tones under the cloudless spring sky.

While his parents chatted quietly to friends and

acquaintances, Francis joined his classmates, standing awk-wardly apart from the other guests, hands in pockets, heads down. No one knew how to behave.

Paul, a classmate he had little time for, greeted Francis with a smirk. "What a surprise. I thought you'd be hanging with the emos."

"What are you talking about?" Francis countered. Paul had always been a pain in the butt.

"Over there." Paul gestured. "Coming your way."

Sawyer and Jack were pushing their way through the crowd toward him. They caught his eye and waved.

Francis took in Sawyer's striped leggings, wild hair, big purple shirt and ruby-red lips. No sign of a baby bump, thank god. Jack looked like he always looked—leather jacket, skinny jeans, long hair, rainbow bangs, and something new—a yellow bruise above his left eye. They were inappropriately dressed for the occasion. He jogged toward them, not ready for his worlds to collide. "I didn't expect to see you here." He chomped down on his lip. "I mean, I'm glad you came."

Jack gave an almost imperceptible nod. He seemed tense. "Sawyer wanted to be here," he said curtly. "I could have given it a miss, but I like Kevin."

"You don't even really know him," Francis retorted.

"Maybe I don't," replied Jack. "I hope he doesn't mind that we're here."

Sawyer poked Jack in the ribs. "Relax. You don't have to be invited to a funeral. We saw your mom and we met your dad, Francis. He's tall. Good genes." She patted her tummy. "They seem okay about the baby. At least, your dad did. Your mom looked sad, but I thought they'd be more freaked out."

Jesus, thought Francis, shooting Jack a helpless look.

"Like she says, relax," Jack said. "Your parents are all right."

Francis changed the subject. "What happened to your eye?"

"My dad happened," Jack replied tersely. "And from what I understand, he was the complete opposite of Kevin's dad. Sad."

The church bells rang out, signaling that the time had come to go inside. "So, I'll catch you guys later?" Francis turned to go.

"Don't you want to sit together?" Sawyer asked.

"Uh…I have to sit with my parents." Francis spotted his mom and dad halfway up the steps, scanning the crowd for him. "They're waiting for me. And I have to go to the reception with them." The implication that Sawyer and Jack wouldn't be welcomed there was not lost on either of them. "Maybe we can hang later on?"

Jack's lips curled into a smirk. "Whatever. Don't worry; we're sitting at the back, so you won't have to explain us to your snotty friends. Come on, Sawyer, let's find a seat." Jack turned on his heel and led Sawyer away, leaving Francis alone with his shame.

When he caught up with his parents, his dad asked if Sawyer and Jack would be sitting with them. Francis, furious with himself for being such a snob, didn't answer. Soft music greeted them as they entered the church.

"Francis?" his mom asked worriedly, "are you okay?" She rested her hands on Francis's shoulders. "I spoke to Sawyer.

She's a wonderful young woman. Honey…" She held his hand, just for a brief second, and smiled. "I've come to terms with your decision—I'll support you. I'm very proud of you."

"Thanks, Mom." His voice broke. "That means everything."

He craned his neck to see the large screen that flashed images of Mr. Croyden's life to the mourners—his marriage to Kevin's mother, holding Kevin as a baby, coaching the soccer team, hoisting Kevin on his wide shoulders, giving a toast at a formal dinner, on water skis, helping Kevin build a Lego spaceship. There was even a shot of Francis clowning around with Mr. C at mini-putt golf. The images went on and on. His mother reached over and took his hand again. He didn't pull away.

Slowly, the Hudson school choir filed in, followed by the black-robed, somber minister, who placed the urn holding Mr. Croyden's ashes on the altar. *Thank God there's no coffin*. Kevin, his face wooden, entered the church from the front, holding his mother's arm. She moved slowly, her hollow eyes dark with grief. The rest of the extended family filed in behind them and sat down in the pews reserved for relatives. They were all dressed in black, and they all wore a sprig of purple lavender to acknowledge Mr. Croyden's love of his herb garden. The service opened with the choir singing one of Bach's Chorales. The hymns had been carefully chosen to celebrate, rather than to mourn, Mr. Croyden's life. Kevin's Uncle James read the eulogy.

Then it was Kevin's turn to speak. When he made his way to the altar, everyone sat forward in the pews. In a steady voice, he recited the poem by Mary Elizabeth Frye he'd chosen:

Do not stand at my grave and weep,
I am not there—I do not sleep.
I am the thousand winds that blow,
I am the diamond glints in snow,
I am the sunlight on ripened grain,
I am the gentle autumn rain.
As you awake with morning's hush
I am the swift-up-flinging rush
Of quiet birds in circling flight.
Do not stand at my grave and cry,
I am not there—I did not die.

Finally, the minister intoned the closing prayer. Everyone filed out of the church to gather in small groups before setting off to the reception at a hotel downtown. Francis searched the crowd for Jack and Sawyer. He spotted them standing apart from everyone, deep in conversation. He broke away from his parents and pushed through the throngs of people. "Hey, Jack, Sawyer," he called. They turned toward him, Jack's eyes fiery and challenging. "So you've decided it's okay to be seen with us?"

"I'm sorry," Francis said simply. "I'd like it if you came to the reception with my family."

Jack laughed. "Not happening."

Sawyer poked him in the ribs. "Don't be so hard on him. He can't help himself."

"What's that supposed to mean?"

"It means," Sawyer explained patiently, "let's hope some of the traits of your dad and Kevin's dad rub off on you one day."

"Point taken," Francis conceded. "I'm not an idiot, you know, even if I seem like one. I'm not feeling especially proud of my behavior the last little while."

Jack offered him his hand. "No problem. Live and learn."

"Thanks. I'm glad you're my friend."

"Okay, enough," Sawyer interjected. "We all agree that Francis can be an ass, but he's improving. New topic. Can you come over tomorrow? My mom is meeting the staff from Phoenix—the adoption agency—this afternoon. They're giving us access to a website listing would-be parents for private adoption. That means we can start the parent search soon."

"Okay."

"And another thing," continued Sawyer, "Kevin had the kind of dad I want for my baby. Ask him if he'd help us. All those things they said about his father—he must have been a great guy—a kind man. Maybe Kevin, of all of us, is the best qualified to pick the most loving parents for London."

"London? Is that her name?" Francis liked it. It was different.

Sawyer beamed. "Isn't it perfect? I guess the new parents might give her another name, but I'm going to ask them to keep it as her middle name."

"I love it." Francis wrapped his arms around her. "My dad says he thinks you are very brave. When we have to say good-bye to London, we're going to know she's in the best hands."

"Oh my god, Jack! Do you remember what that old

woman said to me?" Sawyer didn't wait for him to reply. "*Saying good-bye to London won't be easy, but it's the right thing to do.*"

"And she was right. It is the right thing to do," Jack assured her.

As usual, Francis didn't have a clue as to what they were talking about.

• • •

At the reception, Francis waited until Kevin was alone to approach him with Sawyer's request. "I want you there too," he told him. "After all, if it weren't for you, I'd never have gone to that dance and I would never have met Sawyer."

Kevin looked confused. "Wouldn't that have been better?"

"I would have said the same thing not too long ago, but the truth is, I think this has changed me for the better."

"Was this your idea, or Sawyer's?" Kevin asked suspiciously. "Because I don't need pity from you."

"Sawyer's," Francis replied. "She thinks that you'll recognize a good dad when you see one, because you had a good dad. She's right."

Kevin smiled. "Okay. I'm in. My house is full of a thousand relatives, most of them I don't even know. It stinks of rotting flowers, and Mom walks around like a zombie most of the time."

"Okay. I'll let Sawyer know." Francis pulled out his phone.

"No," Kevin protested. "I'll text her myself."

Francis couldn't hide his surprise. "Really."

"Yeah, really, Francis. While you were busy hating Jack, Sawyer and I became friends. Don't worry. It's platonic, but I like her."

"Okay." Francis held up his hands in surrender. "My mom and dad are ready to go home. We have to save the poor baby-sitter, but meet me at the bus at Broadway and 27th at nine tomorrow morning."

"Why so damn early?"

"It's Saturday. Soccer practice is at two."

"Right. I forgot. I'll be at practice," Kevin promised. "I know my dad would want me to be there."

"Kevin, I got to say good-bye to your dad. You were the most important thing to him. He told me that, and he told me to remind you every so often, so get used to it."

Kevin looked down at the floor. "I appreciate it. You're a good friend. Now, can we go back to normal for a while?"

Francis looked around the crowded room. He rolled his eyes. "There's nothing normal about my life right now. Or yours."

Chapter Fourteen

Like a little fish in the sea, your baby is now "breathing in" amniotic fluid—exercising her lungs for her first breath of air. You might feel her hiccup and she is learning to swallow.

Excerpt: *From Conception to Birth*

The next morning found Sawyer, Jack, Kevin, and Francis bunched up on the couch in Sawyer's small living room, listening to her mother explain how the process would work. "Phoenix Adoption has granted us access to their website, where you'll find profiles of clients who are hoping to become parents. We'll be working with a woman named Ms. Yeung. Sawyer is just over six months pregnant, so although we are in no hurry, the sooner we pick London's parents, the easier it will be for Sawyer to focus on other things, like her health and schoolwork." She gave her daughter a knowing look.

"So, Ms. Yeung suggests we pick three or four possible couples to begin with and then we'll narrow it down to one. Take your time. There are so many people looking for children. Francis and Sawyer, with my help, will interview the candidates and then we'll share the information with Kevin and Jack and vote. Sawyer feels strongly that each one of us has an equal vote. Any questions?"

Kevin and Francis noddd, but Jack had something to say. "Why can't we all be in on the interviews?"

"We considered that," explained Ms. Martin, "but Ms. Yeung felt that might be a bit overwhelming for her clients. I agreed, and so did Sawyer. Most people are intimidated by teenagers, and besides, these people are under a lot of stress. We want to make it as easy for them as possible, okay?" Mrs. Martin smiled, doing her best to make this tough situation easier. "Over to you, Sawyer."

"Thanks, Mom. Before we begin," Sawyer spoke formally, "I have a couple of things to say. We all have something to bring to the table. Me, well, that's kind of obvious. Francis, besides being the dad, has two adopted brothers." She turned her big eyes to Kevin. "Kevin, from everything I know, your dad had all of the qualities of a five-star father. I'm so sorry he's gone." She paused. "And Jack? Jack's my best friend, and his dad, unlike yours"—she glanced ar Kevin—"is everything a father shouldn't be. I'm counting on all of you to use your intuition and experience to pick the right parents for London, and in the end, like my mom said, we'll vote. I've asked Jack to give you some background on this whole process. Jack, go ahead."

He flicked his hair out of his eyes and drew in his breath as he looked down at his notes. "Okay, so basically I've written down the key points—uh, that is, the things we need to know about private adoptions, 'cause that's what ours is." He cleared his throat and Kevin gave him an encouraging nod. "So, you guys"—he jutted his chin toward Sawyer and Francis—"need a medical and social history taken, so the baby's parents will know about your health—any medical information could be important for the baby in the future—background, education, and, most importantly, I think, why you chose to go this route instead of keeping the baby, or, you know…terminating the pregnancy. As far as the prospective parents go, they've already done a ton of work, so keep in mind that this hasn't been easy for them. By the time we get their files, they've already done the following: met five to six times over several months with a Phoenix social worker, had criminal-record checks, had a Ministry of Children and Family Development prior contact check, gathered their personal references, undergone medical check-ups, submitted financial statements, submitted copies of birth, marriage, and, if applicable, divorce certificates. They've also attended a parenting course and weekend education seminars." Jack looked up at his friends and grinned. "In other words, by the time they get to this point in the adoption process, they've been screened and they really want a baby. They are totally committed."

"There's one thing," Sawyer said. "Can I stay in contact with London if I want to?"

If anyone besides Francis noticed her mother's disapproving look, they didn't let on.

"Good question," Jack said. "You can choose to stay in

contact with the baby, or not, and if you want, you can allow the baby to contact you when she is eighteen. That has nothing to do with the adoptive parents. That's your decision.

"The other thing is, once you choose the parents, you still can't sign the adoption papers until the baby is seven days old and—this is important—you can change your mind about the adoption within twenty-one days of her birth."

"Wow!" Francis interjected. "As if it isn't hard enough already. Anything else?"

"Yeah. You'll both have to talk to a lawyer to finalize everything because you're underage. Ms. Yeung will arrange that." He put down his notes. "That's about it."

Sawyer's mom spoke up. "Thank you, Jack. Now, I've printed out a whole set of questions from the agency that we can discuss to help us find the right parents. What if we start there?"

They all agreed, and Mrs. Martin continued. "My question is: What makes great parents?"

Jack's hand shot up. "They don't beat the shit out of you."

"They don't abandon their family," Sawyer called out.

"They make you feel that you are the most important person in their world," Francis offered. "They support you."

Kevin's foot connected hard with the leg of the coffee table. "They don't die on you."

"Okay," said Jack. "This isn't going to be easy for any of us. I wouldn't mind a quick smoke, if we could take a break."

Mrs. Martin stood up. "I'll put on the kettle, but as far as I'm concerned, a good parent loves his or her child unconditionally and has the backbone to guide it through life by example."

"Well put, Mom."

While Jack darted outside for a cigarette, Mrs. Martin made a pot of tea. When Jack returned, Francis thought he looked calmer, happy almost. *He likes this* Francis thought. *We're like family to him.*

"So, moving on," Mrs. Martin said, "do we want to have an open, semi-open, or closed adoption with the adoptive family?"

"Definitions, please," said Francis.

"Closed is when there is no contact between the birth parents and the adoptive parents, and there is no identifying information from either of you, and no communication after the adoption."

Sawyer drew her hand across her throat. "Nix that one."

"Open," Mrs. Martin continued, "is the opposite. The parents and the birth parents have ongoing communication, and all of the information on both sides is shared. You decide how much contact you want and the adoptive parents can be there for the birth."

"I don't know about the rest of you, but I do know that I want them there for the birth. I mean, I'm certainly not going to count on Francis being there."

"Shit," cried Francis. "I hadn't even thought about that yet."

Kevin patted him on his back. "You're kind of pale," he teased.

"A semi-open adoption is somewhere between the two," Mrs. Martin continued, ignoring the exchange. "The biggest difference is that direct communication is limited and always carried out by a third party; in your case, that would be Phoenix. No sharing of names and addresses, but you agree on the frequency of communication. Phew, that's it."

"We haven't even gone beyond the first two questions," pointed out Jack, "and I'm starving."

"Me too," said Kevin.

"Ditto," chimed in Francis.

"Mom said this would happen." Sawyer laughed.

Mrs. Martin disappeared into the kitchen, reappearing moments later with a platter laden with croissants, jam, giant cinnamon buns, and cut-up melons and oranges. "I don't know how your families can afford to feed you," she joked.

While they ate, they talked about the three options. Francis came out strongly in favor of a closed adoption. "I think it would be weird if we knew Nate and Devon's parents."

"Why don't you?" Jack wanted to know.

"They disappeared during the civil war in the Ivory Coast. So many people disappeared…" He sighed. "At first we asked for only one child, but Mom says we were doubly blessed, and I agree with her."

Sawyer preferred the semi-open adoption, and in the end, they agreed (since she had a stronger vote) to open records. But the sharing of letters and photos on the baby's birthdays proved to be a bigger problem.

Mrs. Martin, who was usually so agreeable, thought the idea to be, in her words, "damaging and absolutely untenable." She set her lips in a tight, thin line. "I just can't condone it."

But her daughter was equally stubborn. "I'd be pretty happy to hear from my dad once a year."

"But, sweetheart," Mrs. Martin shook her head sadly, "you had a relationship with your dad. This baby doesn't belong to you. I think your letters will confuse her and cause problems. We have to put her welfare first. You say it all the time."

To everyone's surprise, Sawyer burst into tears. It was Kevin who saved the day. "I know, why don't we agree on the yearly letters and photos, but give the parents the choice to show them to London either when they arrive or on her eighteenth birthday?"

"I could agree to that," said Mrs. Martin. She rubbed her daughter's back gently. "Sawyer?"

"I suppose." Sawyer sniffled. "It's just so hard when you put it like that…"

"Well, you know me. I've never been one to mince words."

"Good," said Kevin, eager to move on. "Now we can tackle the next question on this long list. Do we care about the age of the adoptive couple?"

"No old farts," said Jack. "Like, not older than thirty-five."

"That's not old," said Francis. "That's middle-aged."

"What about thirty-eight?" suggested Sawyer. "Mature—it takes longer to get an education and to get a career established these days."

"Ahem." Sawyer's mother rolled her eyes. "I'm not going to tell you how old I am, but thirty-five is certainly not middle-aged! I think you need to keep an open mind. If we find the perfect couple at forty, we shouldn't write them off."

"Got it," said Kevin, writing down the answer. "Next question: Does it matter if the adoptive family lives in the same city as you do?"

A heated debate followed. Sawyer, Francis, and her mother were dead set against it. Kevin and Jack were indifferent. "As long as she lives in *a* city," said Jack.

"Too restrictive," argued Mrs. Martin. In the end, they all agreed with her.

"Okay, what about income? Rich, poor, doesn't matter?"

"Not poor," put in Jack. "Poor is a whole set of problems on its own."

"They don't have to be uber-rich either." Sawyer gave Francis a sideways glance. "Super-rich people can be snobs."

"Look, I already apologized for that," Francis said. "Can we agree on comfortable and educated?"

Kevin wrote it down. "Next, what about religion?"

That was an easy one for all of them. "No fanatics. No extremes."

"Is it important to you for your child to have siblings?"

"No!" shouted Sawyer.

"Yes!" shouted Francis at exactly the same moment.

"I'm not budging on this one," warned Sawyer, her dark eyes flashing. "I love being an only child."

Francis's chin jutted forward. "I'm not budging either. I love my brothers."

"How about we leave this one to the end?" Jack suggested.

Kevin kept his thoughts to himself, although he'd always wanted a brother or sister. Francis, not wanting to do battle, backed down. "Okay, we can decide later. That's okay by me. You good with that, Sawyer?"

"Whatever," she muttered. "But we're going to have to talk about it sometime."

Kevin pushed on. "Well, here's an easy one: Do you want your child to have a mother *and* a father?"

"Yes," they all chorused.

"I think it's unfair and unwise not to consider a single mom." Mrs. Martin clearly had strong feelings on some subjects. "After all, Sawyer and I are doing very well on our own."

"I agree." Kevin surprised everyone. "I read somewhere that a child only really needs one good parent to turn out well, to feel loved."

"I could have used one of those," Jack interjected. "I agree. We should consider a single mother, but not a single dad."

"Okay." Kevin made a note of it. "We're almost at the end of the list. Would you feel comfortable if a same-sex couple raised your child?"

They all fell silent, contemplating the question. "I wouldn't mind," Sawyer spoke up.

"My feelings should be pretty clear on this one," offered Jack, with a slight smile, "but they're not, even though I'm gay. I miss my mom, even if I never knew her. I wish I had a mom."

Kevin's eyes grew wide. Of course he'd heard the heated exchange between Jack and his father, but he'd put Mr. Meneer's cruel words down to bullying.

Jack cracked up. "Yes, Kevin. I'm gay. What's up with you prep-school guys and your lack of gaydar? I thought it would have been perfected, but wow, was I wrong."

A red flush crawled up Kevin's face. "Sorry, man. And for the record, I see nothing wrong with a same-sex couple. My Uncle James is gay, and he's married to Tom, and they're two of the best guys I know aside from my dad."

"Cool," said Jack. "Francis?"

"Yeah. I can't see anything wrong with that. All I want for this kid is a good family."

Sawyer clapped her hands. "You actually are a nice guy."

"Next," said Kevin, looking at his watch. "We don't have much more time. Our game is in an hour, so we can't stay much longer. Do you want a family where one parent will stay at home?"

That wasn't an issue for anyone.

"So we're back to the sibling question," said Kevin. "I don't have any brothers or sisters, but I wish I did. We know about Nate and Devon. What about you, Jack?"

Jack shook his head. "Just me and Dad. Now just me."

"Sawyer? You feel pretty strongly about this."

"Nah, I'm chill about it now. I get grumpy sometimes. Mostly I care about the mom and dad." She turned to her mother. "I'm feeling kind of tired, Mom."

"Okay." Mrs. Martin jumped up, full of concern for her daughter. "Everybody out. We covered a lot of ground and it's intense stuff. Let's all meet again at the same time tomorrow and go over the different profiles."

She shooed them out the door. When they'd left, she turned to her daughter. "I love you," she said. "And I admire you too."

That night, Sawyer slept deeply, realizing that she had all she needed to be happy—one amazing parent and some very loyal friends.

Chapter Fifteen

By the seventh month, your baby's eyes can
open and close and can sense light changes.
Your baby can also make grasping motions
and likes to suck her thumb.

Excerpt: *From Conception to Birth*

The next evening, the four friends were huddled around
Sawyer's computer, their eyes glued to the screen. Nobody
spoke as Sawyer scrolled through the profiles of prospective
parents.

"There are so many of them," she whispered. "How are we
ever going to pick the perfect mom and dad?"

"Maybe they'll pick us," offered Kevin hopefully. "You
know, just kind of jump off the page."

Francis remained silent, studying Sawyer out of the corner

of his eye. He still couldn't get used to her new roundness. Her tummy left little doubt that the baby's arrival lay only a couple of months off. She was handling it well. She appeared relaxed and positive. Her hair had a sheen to it, and the strain of those initial months had disappeared from her expression. *Good thing too*, he thought, *because Sawyer's moods have a huge impact on how everyone around her feels.*

"Let's hope so. Otherwise, we're screwed." Jack clicked through the pages of people who desperately wanted a child of their own. "It's sad—all these great people who want kids."

For them, the website was a last resort along the bumpy road to parenthood. The pages of detailed profiles laid bare the hopes and dreams of people of all ages and races and beliefs. They wanted the one thing that so many people take for granted—to hear a child call them mommy or daddy.

"It's heartbreaking. They all look so…so…" Sawyer stared at the eager faces, each smiling optimistically toward the camera.

"Ready," Jack finished. "How about if we divide the web pages four ways. Since we've all got our own computers, we can work on our own list. Each of us can pick who we think will be the best candidate from the list we have. One choice only. Okay?"

"Good idea," Kevin agreed. "Then each of us can present our favorite to the group—argue why we think they are the best parents. They have to meet all or most of the criteria we agreed upon."

By the time Mrs. Martin slipped in from work, they were

so engrossed in the task at hand that they failed to hear her enter. "Hello," she called. "Have you made any progress?"

"It's slow." Sawyer yawned. "But we've divided up the parents alphabetically into four groups, and we're not giving up until we find the final four."

"If it's too much for you, sweetheart, you can take a break, or finish up tomorrow."

"I'm okay, Mom."

"Good, then I can't wait to see the couples you come up with."

For the next few hours, they continued to study the profiles. By close to midnight, bleary-eyed and emotionally exhausted, they'd each managed to pick three or four prospective parents. They gave themselves a week to whittle this down to only one and put together their presentations. "That should be enough time, but if you need more, it's okay," Sawyer said.

"So we'll meet back here in seven days." Francis could use the break and figured the others could too.

• • •

Although his parents always tried to be positive when the baby topic arose, Francis knew how difficult it was for them. How hard it would be to say good-bye to their first grandchild. His mother's expression changed (when she thought nobody was looking) from placid to sad, and his father's moods were often punctuated by long, deep sighs. Despite this, Francis's mother helped him to narrow down his top three candidates to one, an impossibly difficult task for her, and he appreciated her help. He'd been surprised—and relieved—when she'd offered her assistance.

"Thanks, Mom." Francis hugged her. "I know how hard this is, and"—his voiced quavered—"well…I'm sorry."

"I want the baby to have the best possible home too." Her eyes filled with tears. "I just wish it didn't have to be this way."

"But it does, Mom. And it's not up to us, anyway," Francis explained again. "It wouldn't be fair to Sawyer."

His dad's approach had been more practical. "We need to consider the baby's future," he insisted. "Think about Devon and Nate and how much we love them. This baby deserves the same love, from adults—not kids still in high school. The twins changed our lives for the better in so many ways. Let this baby do the same for another couple. Please."

"I know you and your dad are right," Francis's mom admitted to him as they sat outside on a sunny afternoon watching Devon and Nate kick a soccer ball around. She smiled. Their high-pitched giggles and happy bantering said it all. "I'm just finding it difficult."

Francis watched his brothers and thought his heart might burst with love. He *knew* they were doing the right thing. Sawyer had made the right choice. His attitude had changed so much since Christmas, and he owed a lot of that change to his father's support.

Things *had* improved at the Sloan household. Although his mother still found discussing the baby hard, her face smoothed, and her smile returned. Francis reverted to being the good big brother he'd always been, once he started to forgive himself and focus on doing the right thing.

His father noticed the change in him. "Francis," he said early one March morning while taking out the trash, "I think you and I need to go for a walk." Francis knew he had something on his mind. "Sawyer is more than two-thirds of the way through her pregnancy," he began. She can no longer disguise her condition. Have you thought about how you're going to handle the boys at school?"

Francis kicked a stone into the gutter. "You know, Sawyer's been open about it since she found out. I can't do that. I just want to keep the whole thing quiet, but if word gets out, well, I'll have to deal with it. I mean, I'll support her. I owe her that."

His dad slowed down and placed his hand on Francis's shoulder. "That's what I hoped you'd say. You know, the measure of a person's character is not the situation he finds himself in, but how he responds to that situation. I probably don't say this often enough. I want to tell you that your mom and I are proud of how you're responding to this whole thing. You've grown up so much. You're not the same angry boy you were in Hawaii. We love you, and we're proud of you."

Francis felt his cheeks redden. "That means a lot, Dad."

They stood facing each other awkwardly. Finally, his dad's serious face broke into a wide grin. "Race you home," he called and set off at a sprint down the street.

Francis watched him lope away. "You don't have a chance," he shouted, but he let his father win.

• • •

All week, Francis devoted his spare time to preparing his presentation. They'd agreed to finalize their choice by the end of March and meet the prospective parents in April. Ms. Yeung had warned them that the selection process and informing the candidates would take time.

Francis felt confident about the couple he'd chosen, and the more he learned about them, the more he liked them. No doubt his friends would be equally passionate about who they wanted to have parent London, so he worked hard to put forth a strong argument. By Thursday night, he felt ready to introduce his choice to the group.

Even so, Francis was anxious the next evening when he arrived at Sawyer's apartment. Looking around at his friends fidgeting with nervous anticipation, he realized they all were. With little fanfare, Mrs. Martin drew names out of a hat to fairly decide the order of the presentations.

"Kevin, you're lucky number one, followed by Sawyer, and then Jack. Last but not least, Francis. So, if you're ready, Kevin, you have the floor."

Kevin groaned. "I always think it's a disadvantage to go first." But his place on the school debating team gave him an edge; he didn't mind public speaking, and it showed. He began confidently. "I'd like to introduce you to David and Beth Scott. They are 'friendly creative, loving, and fun.' David is a high-school math teacher by day, but has a passion for baking. Beth has an organic nursery behind their home, so London would be guaranteed a healthy lifestyle. Beth is thirty-six years old, so slightly older, but not by much. David is thirty-one."

He reached for the file he'd created and pulled out some photos. "Check out the pics I'm about to pass around. Beth bears a freaky resemblance to Sawyer, which would be nice for the baby. She's got the same hair and eye colors. They have a large family—lots of young nephews and nieces, which would also be an advantage for the baby. They live in Kelowna, British Columbia, which, although not a thriving metropolis, is a university town." He nodded at Jack. "So we could call them urban. They write: 'We have a lot of love in our hearts and we can't wait to share our love with your baby or toddler. Please, please consider us.'" Before Kevin sat down, he passed around copies of the Scotts' profile.

Sawyer took his place. "They sound really nice, Kevin, but wait until you meet…Maria Del Ray from Calgary, Alberta. Maria is a single, thirty-seven-year-old woman, divorced, and a veterinarian. I know two-parent families are preferred, but I fell in love with her. She's cool. She lives in a large house in the city and has a black lab called Benny. As you can see from her photo, she's got a tattoo on her left arm, like me. It says: 'Trust in Yourself'—a sentiment I can totally relate to."

She grinned. "I mean, how great is that? A mom with a tat. And a dog. Francis has a dog and he talks to it all the time, so the baby won't be lonely. Anyway, she says: 'I cannot wait to be a mother to the boy or girl I will love with every fiber of my being. Your baby will grow and thrive in an environment of love. He or she will be educated well, travel the world, and gain a deep respect for nature and other people. I admire your courage as a birth mother and am truly grateful that you are reading my profile.'

"She writes that if she were to choose three words to describe how she would treat a child, they would be: 'Love without conditions.' That's a strong statement. Take some time to study her photos and profile and I know you will like what you see."

"It's going to be impossible to choose," Francis said worriedly. "Everyone sounds good."

"It'll be easier once we talk about all of them, but for now, it's Jack's turn," Sawyer said.

Jack switched places with Sawyer. "Beth and David and Maria all sound like loving, kind people, but Michelle and Winston Oliver have all that to offer and more. They are a multicultural couple. Michelle is originally from Paris, France, and her husband of ten years, Winston, is from the Ivory Coast, just like Devon and Nate. He is a writer, a successful one at that, so he is home all day, awesome for a kid. Michelle is a documentary filmmaker. They live in Vancouver in a large apartment in Soho. You can see by their photos that they are pretty active—bike riding, swimming, camping, and skiing. They have a cabin on one of the Gulf Islands.

"Here's what they have to say about themselves: 'We have a lot of love to give and full and happy lives surrounded by family and friends. We want to share our good fortune and joy with a child and we will embrace your baby with open arms and open hearts. He or she will be raised in a fun, creative, bilingual household, with all of the advantages of a full-time at-home parent. Please, take the time to get to know us.' These two meet and possibly exceed our standards. They are both thirty-three years old and both have postgrad degrees. They are ready to start a family and any child would be lucky to call them parents."

He passed around their photos, and everyone agreed that they looked ideal. Then it was time for Francis to present his couple.

So far, he liked all of the possible parents-to-be, but as he took his place in front of his friends, he felt confident in his choice. "Meet Sydney Fox, originally from Vancouver, and Taylor Laberge, from Quebec City. They live in the heart of downtown Montreal. Sydney is thirty-three and Taylor is thirty-five. They are both profs at McGill University. Taylor in anthropology and Sydney in new media studies. Bonus! McGill has a day care on site, and as professors, they keep quite flexible hours. They are bilingual and have a large extended family and tons of support. They spend their summers in the countryside in France. They travel quite a bit.

"This is what they have to say about themselves: 'We love that you are reading our profile and would be overjoyed to welcome a baby into our family. With us, your child will thrive in an environment of love, learning, respect, and joy. Your baby will be cherished. We will speak openly about the adoption and hope that you too might play a part in your child's life.' I don't think I have to add a lot more to that. This couple leapt off the page, and as soon as I read their profile, I knew, hands down, that…that…that our baby deserves a home like this one."

He took a deep breath. "Before I pass out their photos, there is one more thing. They fit most of the criteria, except—and I know you might not approve, Sawyer—they have a three-year-old, a little girl they adopted at the age of one. They want to add to their family. I don't think you should write them off."

He handed the portfolio, including their photo, to Jack. He glanced at it, did a double take, and guffawed. "I didn't expect this at all, not from you." He grinned broadly and passed the pictures on to Kevin.

Kevin's eyes were like saucers. "You're kidding! You're putting forward a gay couple?"

Jack smiled. "Like I said, I never expected this from you, Francis."

Francis ignored them both. He sat down. Then he stood up again and addressed his final plea to Sawyer. "I know you think the baby would be better off without a sibling, but I disagree. I didn't know how lonely I was until we adopted Nate and Devon. There's nothing in the world I wouldn't do for my little brothers. Don't write this family off; at least let them come for the interview before you decide. These are two good dads. And two is better than one." He sat down again. He'd said all he could say.

"Thank you, Francis. Now, there are five of us, including me," said Mrs. Martin. "Let's cast our votes and let Ms. Yeung know the results so she can set up the interviews. Everyone agreed?"

"Yes," they chorused.

"Okay. Why don't you take some time to discuss the candidates while I put together some snacks?"

For the next hour and a half, fortified by sandwiches and sodas, they did just that, poring over the dossiers, photos, and social worker reports, debating the advantages and the disadvantages of each person. Finally, they all agreed they were ready to vote.

"Right," said Mrs. Martin. "Let's start with Kevin's people—David and Beth. A show of hands in favor?"

All four hands shot up. "Okay, David and Beth from Kelowna are in. What about Sawyer's single mom—Maria from Calgary?"

Three hands shot up.

"Against?"

Kevin raised his hand. "She sounds really nice and stable, and I think she could provide a good home for the baby, but I think it's better for a kid to grow up with a dad."

Jack scowled. "Ha. I don't know how you can say that after seeing my father in action!"

Kevin shrugged. "Maybe you'd feel differently if you'd had the chance to see my dad in action," he responded.

Mrs. Martin interrupted. "Sorry, Jack. It's three to one, so Maria is in. Now what about Jack's Michelle and Winston, the bilingual couple from Vancouver?"

Jack raised his hand, followed by Kevin. "That's two for. Against?"

Sawyer and Francis raised their hands.

"We have a tie." Mrs. Martin frowned. "So I guess it's up to me, if everyone agrees?"

They did, sitting on the edge of their seats while Mrs. Martin reviewed the files. At last she spoke. "Sorry, Sawyer, but I agree with Jack and Kevin on this one—they do live a little too close and the risk of running into them is very real. Nonetheless, I'd like to meet them."

Jack's face lit up. "So my couple is in?"

"Yes, even though they are geographically compromised. So finally we have Francis's couple with the little girl. For?"

Francis, Jack, and Kevin raised their hands. "Against? Sorry, Sawyer, but you are outnumbered. That's it, then. I'll contact Ms. Yeung and she'll book the interviews. The sooner the better."

"I couldn't agree more." Sawyer stood up and stretched. "I'm going to feel a lot better when I know who will be parenting my baby."

"Our baby," Francis corrected.

"Wow," Sawyer exclaimed. "You've come a long way!" She shot him a brilliant smile. For the first time in weeks, Francis felt happy.

Chapter Sixteen

In the eighth month, your baby is about 18
inches (45 cm) long and weighs 5 pounds (2
to 2.5 kg). Your baby's kicks are strong and
you may be able to see the outline of a small
heel or elbow pressed against your abdomen.

Excerpt: *From Conception to Birth*

The Phoenix representative, Ms. Yeung, successfully arranged
for all of the prospective parents to be in Vancouver for the
interviews during the first weekend in April.

At first Sawyer was crestfallen. "That's three weeks away,"
she groaned. "I'll be huge!"

"The time will pass quickly," Jack assured her. "Between
school and other activities, it'll fly by."

And it did, but not without challenges. Now into her

eighth month, Sawyer could no longer disguise her growing belly. She'd popped. Her pregnancy was no longer a secret. The kids at her school had started to give her curious looks. Sometimes she heard them whispering about her, or they'd stop talking when she entered the room. She knew she'd have to do something about that—and soon.

One afternoon, when she and Jack were sitting on the couch doing their homework, the baby kicked. Sawyer laughed and Jack eyed her with a raised brow. "What?" he asked, throwing down his pen. "It's impossible to concentrate."

"The baby is really active today," she explained.

"Do you mind?" Jack put his hand on her tummy.

Sawyer smiled. "No, but she doesn't kick on command. You might have to wait forever."

"I've got time," Jack said, but the words were hardly out of his mouth when the baby kicked again, hard. "Wow!" Jack exclaimed. "That is so cool."

Sawyer pushed his hand away. She burst into tears. "I'm afraid of so many things," she cried.

Jack looked at her in astonishment. She'd always been the strong one. She'd always been his rock. He reached out and took her hand, his eyes glued to hers. "What are you afraid of?" he asked softly. "Tell me." He pushed a strand of hair from her cheek and handed her a tissue. "But first blow your nose and take a few deep breaths. I know this is hard."

Sawyer took the tissue. "Thanks," she said, sniffling. "I don't know what I'd do without you."

"Well, seeing as I'm still living on your couch," Jack said, laughing, "I guess you could say that the feeling is mutual. Now, what's bothering you?"

She hesitated, taking a deep breath. "What if I can't do this? What if it hurts too much? What if the baby hates her new family and then hates me her whole life?" Once again her eyes filled with tears. "I didn't expect to feel so guilty. And I hate the way the kids at school stare at me when they think I won't notice."

"Whew," Jack said, pulling her into his arms. "That's a lot of shit, but I think I can help you out. You can do this. I know you can, and there are drugs that you can take during childbirth that will make it easier. Trust me, I've been reading up on the whole thing. It's going to be hard for you, harder for you than anyone, to give the baby to a new family, but she will love you for it. She will understand. Don't feel guilty about doing the right thing."

"Okay." Sawyer sniffled again. "Okay. But sometimes it's hard to remember I'm doing the right thing."

Jack kissed her on the forehead. "It's funny. We all thought you were cool with the kids at school. You hide your real feelings pretty well. You should talk to someone, a teacher you can trust. Hold your head high, because you *are* doing the right thing." Sawyer blew her nose. "Easy for you to say."

Jack kept his voice level. "No. You're wrong. It's not easy for me to say, and it's been even harder for me to do. I'm gay, Sawyer. Remember? Coming out was a nightmare. But it felt good too, no more hiding. No more pretences. But don't kid yourself; I've been bullied and mocked and beaten up," he said. "Even by my own dad."

His voice trembled slightly. "When I think that my dad disowned me, it kills me, but I've never once doubted my choice."

"And you shouldn't," Sawyer said.

Jack smiled. "It's no different for you, Sawyer. Now you have to be strong. There's no hiding the fact that there's a kid growing inside of you, so do the right thing. It's one sure way of finding out who your real friends are."

Of course he was right. She put her arms around his neck and hugged him. "Thank you, Jack."

• • •

Instead of her usual oversized shirt, Sawyer dressed for school the next day in a pretty purple shirt that hugged her belly. When her classmates and other kids in the school saw her bump, some tittered, some made rude remarks, while others turned away, embarrassed. It hurt a bit, but she tried hard to ignore them and concentrate on her work. At break, she waited until all the students had left the room, then approached Miss Addison. "There's something I have to tell you," she said. "I mean, obviously I'm pregnant, but I want to talk about it—like be open and everything."

"I'd hoped you'd talk to me." Miss Addison got up and closed the classroom door. "You've been putting up with the reactions of your classmates, but by confiding in me, I think I can take advantage of what we call teachable moments."

"I'd feel better if we could talk about it openly," Sawyer

confessed. "I'm tired of kids staring at me as if I'm some kind of circus act."

"Actually, they're just curious, but I can see how it might feel that way. Many of them think that what you're doing is pretty amazing."

"Really?"

"Really," Miss Addison reassured her. "You're not the first young girl to get pregnant. Sadly, you won't be the last. Thank you for trusting me, Sawyer. Now, with your permission, I'll talk to your other teachers and to the students in this class. Don't worry; when I'm finished with them, they will have nothing but admiration for you. I hope they'll learn how to avoid finding themselves in a similar situation too. You're a brave girl, and you are doing the best you can under the circumstances. Hold your head high, and nobody will question you. If they do, be honest."

Not trusting herself to speak, Sawyer simply nodded. She'd been so nervous about approaching Miss Addison, but Jack had been right. She hadn't realized that her teacher saw her as a brave girl and not a fool.

• • •

A week before the parent interviews, Francis turned sixteen. On the same day, he successfully passed his driving test, earning his learner's license.

"I guess if I can trust you behind the wheel," his dad joked, "you're old enough to drive this fixer-upper." He presented

Francis with the keys to a little gray four-door Toyota station wagon, while his mother snapped pictures and his brothers circled him in excitement, demanding rides. "It's not new, just about ten years old," his dad explained. I've been working on it off and on with Ted." Ted, Francis knew, was one of his dad's pilot friends and he was handy with wrenches.

"Thanks, you guys. I never expected this!"

"Let's go." Nate grabbed Francis's hand.

Francis picked up his little brother and swung him through the air. "I've only got my learner's so I can't drive you guys. Only family members twenty-five and over with a valid driver's license."

"We won't tell anyone," Devon protested.

"Because there will be nothing to tell," their mother announced, shooing them into the house. "Now, it's time for cake. Maybe Francis will let you help him to blow out the candles."

That afternoon, Francis met Kevin and Jack at the movie theater, where they filled themselves with popcorn and soda before heading out for ice cream after the show. *It all feels so normal*, Francis thought, and he wished it could last forever. But how could it, when he knew that, within weeks, he would be a dad? *Not a real dad*, he corrected himself, *but a dad, nonetheless.*

Jack noticed his sudden withdrawal and elbowed him in the ribs. "Hey, what's up? You're suddenly awfully quiet."

Francis smiled faintly. "I'm so damn freaked out about this whole father thing. I can't get my head around it. Sometimes it feels like I've fucked up so badly…"

"Think of it this way," Jack suggested. "We're all dads to this kid in a way, sharing the load."

"Yeah, I guess. Thanks, Jack." Still, Francis knew that it would be him, not his friends, who might have to face this child one day. It would be Francis, not Jack or Kevin, who would have to explain why he'd chosen to say good-bye to London.

The next morning, Francis's father suggested a drive. Francis readily agreed. He needed a distraction, something to take his mind off Sawyer and the baby. Climbing into the driver's seat, his mind was miles away when he pushed the car into reverse and began to back up.

"Stop!" his dad bellowed.

"Shit!" Francis slammed on the brakes.

"You didn't do a shoulder check or look in your mirrors. The boys' bikes are behind the car, but it could have been one of them!"

"I'm sorry, Dad."

"Are you okay, Francis? You seem preoccupied."

"I'm fine," Francis lied.

His dad's eyebrows lifted. "Want to talk about it—after you move the bikes and reverse out of here safely?"

He did as instructed without incident, and they set off down the quiet side streets. At first Francis focused solely on driving, but as he relaxed, he felt the need to talk. "It's nothing really. Only that, what if the baby looks me up when I'm old? What am I supposed to tell her?"

"Ah…it's a good question. You might want to consider writing a letter to London. She'll read it one day, and I know it will mean a lot to her. I wish your brothers had one to look forward to, but, of course, their birth parents are gone."

"We've already agreed that I'm going to write to her every year on her birthday; both Sawyer and I are."

"I know, and I think it's a good idea, but this one will be special. Make it a letter she can't open until she's eighteen. And for god's sake, keep your eyes on the road while we're talking."

"Okay. That way she'll have the answers to her questions as soon as she needs them."

"And she can decide in her own time if she wants to contact you or not, but at least she'll know she was loved from the very start. Sometimes that is enough."

When Francis told Sawyer what his dad had advised, she loved the idea so much that she decided to do the same. "And let's include photos of ourselves, so she knows what we looked like. Sort of like a time capsule for her when she is close to our age." Mrs. Martin even said she'd like to include a note.

"My dad left me a video. Well, actually, he left me five…" Kevin gulped when Francis told him about their plans. He looked away at an invisible spot on the ground. "One for my high-school grad, one for my university grad, one for when I get married, one for my first child, and one to watch when I get to be forty-five—his age when he died."

"Wow." Jack's eyes widened. "I know your dad's gone, Kevin, but I'd take a week with a man like that over a lifetime with the asshole who fathered me. Don't ever forget that. After all, you saw him in action. That's amazing."

Kevin smiled. "He was a good guy, wasn't he, Francis?"

"The best. The kind of dad we want for London. He'll be on my mind when I'm listening to our prospects."

• • •

Sawyer's once-flat stomach boasted a respectably sized baby bump now, and as a result of her constant checkups, vitamins, and better diet, her face had filled out. Francis thought she looked radiant. Obviously she felt a lot better too. No more eating at Joe's convenience store. The morning sickness that had plagued her for the first months of her pregnancy had long since disappeared.

Francis admired the way she continued in school, keeping her top-of-the-class marks. He didn't know she'd been afraid to talk about the baby to her classmates, and he thought it was pretty radical when she started updating her Facebook status about London's growth on a weekly basis.

"I could never do that," he confessed as they sat talking in her apartment. "I never speak about it with my friends at school, even though I think they all know."

"It's not so bad," she told him. "And impossible to hide, anyway. There were a few bitchy comments when they first found out, and a few good ones too. Actually, the kids were pretty supportive and curious. My teacher even did a whole unit on teen pregnancy, and believe me, *everyone* knows *everything* there is to know about birth control. Nobody in my class will end up like this! In fact, most of them probably won't have sex for eons. I wrote a piece about being pregnant. Do you want to see it? It's short and pretty personal, but I showed my teacher and she asked if she could read it to the class. I agreed, so I guess it won't hurt if you see it."

"Sure, why not." Francis took the sheet of paper and began to read.

I never meant for this to happen. When I first found out about the baby, I was so angry and upset and I didn't know what to do or who to turn to. I cried myself to sleep every night for a whole month, but in the daytime, around people, I tried to pretend I didn't really care. But I did and I still do. And some nights, I still cry myself to sleep. At first I blamed my boyfriend. After all, would it have killed him to use a condom or even suggest some kind of birth control? I wanted to talk to him about it, but every time I tried, we got interrupted and then it was too late. He never talked about it, and I was mad, but then I figured out that he was just a kid, even more than I was, and I knew I could have just as easily used protection. I try not to think of the baby as my baby, because she's not, but when she kicks, she kicks a hole right in my heart. I hope she'll forgive me one day. I decided to give her up because I can't look after her the way she deserves to be cared for. I hope she'll understand. I've learned a few things, but the most important advice I have for you is this: It's way easier to get pregnant than to be pregnant. It's easier to give birth than it is to be a parent. I know lots of you are in relationships, so remember my words if you ever decide to play the odds. Even if I never see my baby after she is born, she'll be in my heart until I die. It's not going to be easy living like that, so learn from my mistake.

Francis finished reading and looked at Sawyer. "I know I screwed up," he said softly. "And I never apologized properly for my part in all of this, but I am sorry."

Sawyer's dark eyes widened with pleasure. "Thanks. That means more than you'll ever know. We can't turn back the clock, but we can do the right thing now."

Francis gulped. He found it hard to talk about his feelings, but that didn't stop him from trying. "Sometimes I can hardly bear to think about it. I pretend I'm okay too, but I'm not really. My mom can barely look me in the eye, and my little brothers think I'm great, but I'm not. I'm a shit."

Sawyer knew how hard admitting this was for Francis and did her best to lighten the mood. "Those fun times on the couch really messed up things, didn't they?"

"Yeah. You can say that again."

"But we can't feel sorry for ourselves, Francis. We have to do the best thing for the baby, right?" She stood up and stretched her arms over her head. "No going back."

In school, although it hadn't been easy at first, Sawyer held her head high. She'd learned not to mind talking about the whole pregnancy experience with her classmates, and once she found her confidence, no one could take it away. She didn't have much time left before she faced what she knew would be the most difficult and biggest hurdle in her life. She no longer feared the birth, nor did she doubt her decision. She just hoped she could be as brave as everyone thought she was when it came time to hand her baby over to its new parents. The baby had made its presence known, turning and kicking. Kevin, Jack, and

Francis had felt her movements beneath their nervous hands. She affectionately referred to Baby London as The Alien.

• • •

As Jack predicted, time flew, and suddenly the big meet-the-parents weekend loomed only a few sleeps away. They'd met the week before the interviews to go over their questions.

Ms. Yeung sent a short, heartening email urging them to relax and really try to get to know the candidates. "Ask them anything you want," she encouraged. "And if you have any questions beforehand, please call or email me. You'll meet David and Beth Scott on Saturday morning. In the afternoon, Michelle and Winston Oliver. On Sunday morning, Maria Del Ray will be first, followed by Sydney Fox and Taylor Laberge. Please keep in mind that these people are under a lot of stress. Some of them have been trying to adopt for years. It's an arduous journey. Be kind, and good luck!"

Chapter Seventeen

You've reached full-term. Your baby can now
survive outside the womb. Your baby is able
to identify your voice and knows your favorite
music. She is about the size of a honeydew
melon.

Excerpt: *From Conception to Birth*

Ms. Yeung had scheduled the interviews with ample time
between each one. She'd purposely spread the two-hour
meetings over the weekend to make travel easier and so that
no one would have to take time off work or school.

Unbeknownst to each other, all seven of the hopeful parents-to-be found themselves at Vancouver airport's arrivals area
on the Friday morning preceding the interviews. Coincidently,
five of them had flown in on the same flight from Calgary. The

others, Taylor, Sydney, and their little girl, Star, touched down from Montreal five minutes after the Calgary flight.

The Calgary flight had made one stop in Kelowna, British Columbia, before continuing on to Vancouver. The magnificent Okanogan Lake appeared to be blanketed with diamonds—a combination of light and unseasonably warm sunshine on its calm surface.

Maria—Sawyer's choice—glanced out the window only briefly. Uncharacteristically, she had little interest in the vista spread out below her. Instead, her mind remained focused on the upcoming interview that could change her life forever. She found it somewhat intimidating that her suitability as a mother would be decided by a young teenaged girl, the girl's mother, and the biological father, who was still a child himself.

"It's unusual," Ms. Yeung agreed, "but Sawyer is the biological mother, and we have to respect her wishes and the wishes of those she's chosen to help her with this tough decision. Don't worry. I'm sure you'll be able to answer all of their questions. They'll love you." Ms. Yeung meant it. Maria was a lovely woman with all of the attributes of a great parent.

She'd said similar things to two of the other four sets of prospective parents—an odd mix certainly, but overall, the kids had chosen fine candidates. Ms. Yeung did harbor some reservations about one couple, but they'd passed the home study with flying colors, their references checked out, and there were no red flags—being the professional that she was, she kept her personal feelings private. She felt confidant Sawyer Martin and her friends would also have doubts and eliminate the couple in question. If not, so be it. It was, after all, up the bio-mom and not the facilitator to make the final decision.

For her part, Maria desperately wanted to believe Ms. Yeung; however, she didn't allow herself to be overly optimistic. Since she'd begun the arduous process of adoption, she'd learned that her single status weighed heavily against her, so she did her best to keep her emotions in check. After all, she reasoned, the higher her hopes, the harder her fall. She'd been surprised—no, elated—when the phone rang with the unexpected news that she'd been chosen as a possible parent candidate in a domestic adoption.

She'd almost said no, fearful that she'd have to face yet another disappointment. She'd been on both the foreign and domestic adoption lists for four years. She could count on one hand the number of countries whose agencies would allow single-parent adoptions. She'd even had offers from Lesotho and the Ivory Coast, but both had been withdrawn due to civil unrest and new governments—the last-minute denials had nearly broken her.

And now this. The call she'd been praying for. It hadn't been easy to leave her practice on such short notice, but she'd found a retired veterinarian willing to take over the clinic for three days. Better yet, he'd agreed to look after Benny, her lovable Lab.

Two rows behind Maria, two equally anxious people, Michelle and Winston Oliver, gazed out the small window at the sparkling water below. They'd been in Calgary visiting relatives but were flying home a couple of days earlier than planned

because of the interview with Sawyer. Winston glanced sur-
reptitiously at his wife, unable to curb the anxiety in the pit
of his stomach. He felt ambiguous about the interview. The
strain of a four-year search for a child had begun to show on
his wife's face. Fine lines creased the area around her cat-green
eyes and the corners of her mouth. They'd tried everything—
in vitro fertilization, overseas adoption, foster care, and now
this—the possibility of a newborn on the other side of the
Rocky Mountains. He refused to get his hopes up. Like Maria,
there had been too many disappointments, too many tears. He
worried about how much more his wife could handle.

"*Ça va, cherie?*" She had not let go of his hand the whole
flight. She smiled weakly and rested her head on his shoulder.

"I'm terrified. What if they don't like us? What if they like
the other couples better?"

Winston didn't want to think about that. "*Ce qui sera, sera,
cherie.*" He kissed the top of her head. "All we can do is meet
them, and after that, it's out of our hands."

She sighed and tapped her foot impatiently. "How long
until we arrive?"

"Thirty-five minutes. We'll be in Vancouver within the
hour. Besides, we don't meet the kids until Saturday afternoon.
Perhaps we can enjoy a dinner out this evening and a walk
around the seawall in the morning."

"Perhaps," she replied, but she didn't sound at all enthusiastic. "I'd prefer to eat at home tonight, if that's okay with you."

"*Bien sûr.* Of course. I'll make something delicious, and
we'll watch a movie."

Half a dozen people deplaned in Kelowna and another six or seven got on. Michelle studied the new passengers absently, catching the eye of a sturdy thirty-something woman decked out in a tentlike flowered dress and flat, plain sandals. She had a massive carry-on bag, the words *Drink Kelowna Wine* stitched in on both sides. Her laden-down companion, probably her husband, took up the rear, maneuvering a similar carry-on bag.

"Be careful with my stuff, David," the woman barked.

He noticed Michelle watching them and smiled as if to say *I just do what I'm told*.

Michelle grinned, temporarily distracted from her own worries. It took all kinds. For a minute, she let herself hope, but then she cut off her thoughts. *I don't know if I can stand losing another child. Think about other things...*

Twenty minutes later, they were airborne. The short flight left no time for snacks, and the flight attendants had barely finished their drink service before everyone had to buckle up for the approach to Vancouver.

The woman in the tent dress turned to her travel companion, David, and crossed herself. "I hate landing." Her voice carried half the length of the airplane.

David shrugged. "It's in God's hand, Beth. No use worrying." It was wishful thinking because, in his mind, Beth did little else. Maybe a baby would distract her from her daily anxieties, but he doubted that. A child would be nice, but he'd be happy continuing on with their double income and uncomplicated lifestyle.

Beth interrupted his thoughts. "You'll have to shave before we meet the girl. We'll buy you a new golf shirt. You've had that one for years and it looks worn."

David nodded. "Don't worry. I'll put my best foot forward."

"You'd better. I'm counting on you." It sounded like a threat.

As the wheels hit the runway, Beth closed her eyes and her lips moved feverishly in prayer. Beth didn't have much faith in her husband, but she knew she could count on God.

Eleven a.m. was a busy time at Vancouver International Airport. Four flights landed within minutes of each other, and the passengers waited impatiently to pick up their bags. After a long delay, a disembodied voice announced: "Flight 247 arriving from Kelowna: your bags will be on carousel three. Flight 898 from Montreal: your bags will be on carousel four."

"That's us." Taylor made a beeline for carousel four, while Sydney and three-year-old Star went in search of a baggage cart. Taylor watched the two walk away. At six four, with a crop of dark, curly hair, holding sleepy Star's hand, his partner stood out in the crowd of travelers. Taylor loved everything about Sydney, but mostly he loved Sydney's enthusiasm, even after their many years together. Another baby, he mused, meant more joy for their family. They'd flown in two days early, planning to visit friends and sightsee before their meeting with the baby's mom and her friends on Sunday. Both he and Sydney loved the idea of being interviewed by a couple of teens and the grandmother.

On the way to the carousel, Sydney bumped into a well-dressed woman clutching the hand of a tall, handsome black man. "*Pardon*." He'd reverted to his native French.

"*De rien*," she responded, her accent perfectly Parisian.

Her husband smiled at Sydney. "*C'est un peu fou ici, non?*"

Sydney nodded. "*Un peu*." He couldn't wait to get their bags and head out on an adventure. Once outside, they joined a long line of people waiting for cabs.

In front of them, Sydney noticed the multiracial couple he had exchanged pleasantries with at the baggage carousel; while behind them, a rather loud, oddly dressed couple argued about the price of a cab versus a hotel shuttle.

"We could save twenty-five dollars and take the Canada Line," the scruffy, thin man argued. "That's twenty-five dollars better spent on a nice meal. Come on, Beth. Can't you listen to me for once?"

"No, David. My feet are swollen from the flight, and we've got too many bags. We're taking a cab, and that's all there is to it."

Sydney nudged Taylor. "*Le pauvre*," he whispered. His eyes crinkled and Star giggled—she found her parents' happiness contagious.

At the front of the long line, Maria overheard the same exchange and, not for the first time, told herself that it was better to be single and happy than married and miserable. "Hotel Vancouver," she directed the cab driver. During the twenty-minute drive downtown, she thought about her interview the next day and prayed to a god she didn't believe in to help her become the mother of this unborn child.

At the same time, in different cabs, six other people, all desperate for a child and all hoping to become parents to Sawyer's unborn baby, prayed for exactly the same outcome.

Chapter Eighteen

The weekend of the interviews had finally arrived. Over the next two days, Sawyer would meet the people who would become her baby's parents. It was frightening to think that she held their future in her hands. It was scarier still to realize that her baby's well-being depended on making the right choice.

On Saturday morning, Francis was at Sawyer's house by nine, sleepy but excited. His mother had sent fresh rolls, a fruit tray, croissants, and a bouquet of flowers. Jack's boss supplemented the feast with tea for Sawyer and a carafe of coffee, along with the promise of endless refills for the weekend. Jack set everything up in the kitchen, then hurried out the door. "I'll see you after work," he called. "Good luck."

While they waited for the Scotts to show up, Francis killed time playing video games. Sawyer changed her outfit three times: purple leggings, pink leggings, then finally black.

She seemed tense, but so did her normally unshakable mother, who occupied herself vacuuming and re-vacuuming the small apartment. She also rearranged the flowers three times, until Sawyer ordered her to chill.

"Don't bug me, Sawyer. I want them to feel at home. If I'm nervous, then you can bet that they are three times as nervous."

• • •

David and Beth Scott parked their rental car a block away from the address they'd been given and debated whether to go for a coffee, or simply wait in the car. David had thought it extravagant to rent a car, but Beth thought it tacky to show up by bus for such an important occasion. When they got to Main Street, she regretted her decision. "It's a bit shabby around here," she declared, used to their cookie-cutter subdivision home.

"I like it," David countered.

"You would, wouldn't you?"

They were half an hour early for their interview, as Beth had said they would be, but as usual, David had refused to listen. *Well, that will all change with parenthood*, Beth brooded. He'd have no choice, because although he considered himself to be an expert in most things, she'd read every book under the sun on parenting, and she watched parenting reality TV on a regular basis.

The cold, wet spring temperature did little to dispel Beth's already-cranky mood. She hated the city, certainly no place to raise a child. Kelowna wasn't a city, not really. With a population of just under 180,000, it offered the best of both worlds.

David glanced meekly at his wife. Beth had not slept well at the hotel; she never did when they were away from home—that's why she was so out of sorts, that and the inevitable anxiety. David's heart sank; he knew they looked much better on paper. In real life, they were a despondent, bitter couple, the result of four stressful years trying everything possible to have a child. And failing.

Even though Pastor Jim told Beth that conception lay in God's hands, she refused to give up on her dream of motherhood. David would have been content to accept God's will, but since Beth's will outweighed their Lord's by a heavy margin, he went along with her.

"Do you want to go for a coffee, Beth?" he asked again. "That looks like a nice place on the corner." He tried to keep his voice neutral, though he found her incessant tapping on the steering wheel unbearable. "It might calm your nerves."

"Since when does caffeine act as a relaxant? I think *you* want a coffee. Very well," she huffed. "It's better than sitting here freezing to death." She slammed the door of the car. "Make sure you put money in the meter for the full two and a half hours. I don't want to interrupt the interview, and I don't want to be towed or get a ticket."

By the time she'd organized herself, he'd put money in the meter, and they'd bickered about which coffee shop they'd go to, they no longer had time for coffee. Instead, they plodded over the wet sidewalk to Sawyer's front door. For the first time, Beth allowed some of her nervousness to show on her face. She wanted this baby so very much. They climbed the steps to the third floor and Beth insisted that they stand outside the door for a full five minutes so that she could erase the doubt from her features and try to project some semblance of calm. Finally, she granted David permission to knock.

Mrs. Martin answered the door. "Hello." She stepped aside for them to enter. *My god*, she thought to herself, *they don't look anything like their photos!* "Come in," she said invitingly, forcing her lips into a smile.

The front door was visible from the living room, where the kids sat in nervous anticipation. With Sawyer sitting on the couch, hands between her knees, and Francis on one of the kitchen chairs he'd dragged into the living room, there was little space left for Beth, David and Mrs. Martin to squeeze in. "Please come in and let me introduce you to Sawyer and Francis."

Sawyer jumped up, and Francis followed. Mrs. Martin sat on the arm of the couch. After some initial chitchat, she spoke. "Well, here we all are. I guess we should begin. Sawyer, would you like to start?"

"Well," Sawyer began, "we thought maybe you could tell us a little bit about yourselves—basic things about your everyday lives and how a baby might fit into that scenario." She gulped. In her mind, she'd already decided against them.

David cleared his throat. "Yes, well, I'm a teacher of high-school math, so I have great hours and love kids." He smiled tentatively. "I would teach your baby to bake, because that is my second love."

"And I am an organic gardener," Beth said. "I am home all day, so we'd never need day care. I don't believe in day care. Your baby would be raised on healthy food, and she'd know where that food comes from. We're also members of the Church of God, and she would have a rich spiritual life."

"My wife, well, both of us, really, have wanted a baby for a long time, but God has had his own plans for us, so we've decided to go the adoption route," David explained.

"What about discipline?" Francis already hated them. Kevin would be crestfallen.

"We believe a child needs structure, and, of course, we'd lead by example. We'd make sure she had the right kind of friends and teach her to respect others."

"And herself," Francis added drolly. "Would you want her to respect herself?"

"Of course," snapped Beth. "The teachings of Jesus show us that."

Sawyer giggled. The interview went downhill from there and ended forty minutes early.

"Nightmare!" Sawyer's mother said the minute the couple was whisked out the door. "They are nothing like the online profile. They sounded so...so fanatical."

"We have a rich spiritual life," Sawyer mimicked. "One down and crossed off the list. Three to go."

"Oh god," her mother groaned. "Let's hope it gets better, not worse. They were horrifying. That poor man. At the same time, I think you are all being a tad judgmental about religion. You can't fault people because their beliefs don't align with your own."

Sawyer dismissed her. "Francis, you'd better call Kevin and let him know what happened."

"I will," Francis said. "He'll be disappointed."

At three o'clock, Michelle and Winston, Jack's candidates, took their seats in the chairs vacated by Beth and David. Sawyer, her mom, and Francis liked them immediately. Winston exuded warmth, and Michelle's bright eyes and soft voice betrayed a vulnerable honesty. They held hands. Michelle asked if she could feel Sawyer's tummy, and when the baby kicked, her eyes welled up. "I think she will be beautiful like her mother and tall like her father. No?"

"What will you tell the baby about her adoption, about the birth family?" Francis asked, eager to get on with the interview and skip the preliminaries.

Winston's face lit up. He looked at Michelle. She nodded, trusting his words. "Your baby will know the love in this room. We will tell her that you were very young when you had her and that you wanted the best for her. Of course, every year, she will receive your letters and photos, and she will tell you all about her life. There will be no secrets, no shame."

"Are you religious?" Francis asked nervously, Beth and David still at the forefront of his mind.

Michelle focused her large green eyes on his. Although she did her best to be calm, she tapped her leg with her fingers.

Mrs. Martin felt a wave of sympathy for her. "Michelle," she said kindly, "there are no right or wrong answers. We are gathering information to help Sawyer with her decision."

Her husband squeezed her hand and Michelle let her breath out slowly. "Thank you, Mrs. Martin. You probably understand how hard this is for us. We want a baby so badly…"

Her sentence trailed off, and they all waited patiently for her answer. "We do not attend a church. We are not dogmatic people, but we believe that if one respects oneself, one, in turn, will respect others. We believe that we are all equal and that we are stewards of this planet.

"Your baby will travel the world and will learn these lessons. She will be bilingual, as we have a large family in France as well as in Montreal." Winston laughed, delighted at the thought of what the future might hold.

"Do you have pets?" asked Mrs. Martin.

"We'd like to get a puppy, but not until the baby is old enough to play with it."

They talked about their corner apartment and the bright, yellow room they'd prepared for a child. Mrs. Martin's heart went out to them as she imagined the empty nursery they faced daily. They described in detail their careers, their love of reading, and how they hoped to pass that on to their child. They wanted to know Sawyer's favorite books and music.

"Ska," Sawyer answered. "And I like classical, as well as show soundtracks from musicals too, like *Rent* or *Les Mis*."

"I can play them for the baby, and also opera," Michelle offered.

When Mrs. Martin asked about their history, they explained their years of trying to get pregnant, the in vitro that failed, the roller coaster of emotions they'd experienced; and the more they spoke about themselves, the more likable they became. The only hitch revolved around the baby's name. They reluctantly agreed to London, although they jokingly said they'd prefer Paris. Sawyer suspected London would be given a nickname directly following her birth. It was a small thing, she knew, but it bugged her.

Francis asked, "Winston, who is your role model for a father?"

Winston didn't hesitate. "Ben Parker."

Francis beamed. "Are you kidding me? Excellent!"

Sawyer leaned forward in her chair. "Who?"

"Peter Parker's dad." Francis scoffed. "Peter Parker, aka Spiderman? His uncle Ben and Aunt Mary adopted Peter when his parents were killed in a plane crash. They loved him unconditionally, and 'Uncle' Ben was an awesome dad. He adored Peter. He died." Francis thought of Kevin. "Tragic. Peter was devastated."

"That is right," said Winston. "If not for his Uncle Ben, Peter might have used his powers for evil, but he didn't, because he was so loved. And London will be too."

"We would be honored if you'd allow us to be at her birth—that is, if you select us." Michelle smiled.

The two hours they'd set aside for the interview flew by, and all too soon, Michelle and Winston said good-bye. When they left the apartment, their footsteps were much lighter, and their hearts brimmed with hope for a baby.

"They were a thousand times better than David and Beth," Francis observed. "Definitely front-runners. Winston would be an incredible dad. I mean, totally hands-on and no yelling, and he likes Marvel Comics. Jack did a good job on those two."

"Yes," Sawyer agreed. "What do you think, Mom?"

"I liked them," her mother replied. She had one big concern, but she decided to bring it up when it was time to vote. "Let's wait until we've met them all to decide."

"I think you can safely tell Phoenix that David and Beth are out," Francis said with a laugh. "Boy, did Kevin ever misread those two. We all did."

"I agree," said Sawyer. "But we have to wait until we meet all of them and talk to Jack and Kevin before we call the agency." She hugged him. "That's why there are four of us on the panel. By the way, what did you think about their request to be at the birth?"

Francis grinned. "I think it said a lot. The other two never even brought it up."

"Guess who else wants to be there," Sawyer said.

"Who?" Both Francis and Mrs. Martin spoke at the same time.

"Jack! And I think it's cool, but I said no. Actually, I said no frigging way. You, Mom, you're my birth coach, and I want the nurses, doctors, and the new parents there. That's it."

"I'll hang in the waiting room with Kevin and Jack. Someone can give us the play-by-play. I don't have a problem with that," Francis said.

Sawyer nodded. "Actually, I was hoping you'd say that. You guys can supply food in the waiting room. Deal?"

"Deal. Now, I'm going home. I'm wiped. Will you let Jack know he did a good job of screening his choice?"

"You bet. He'll be here anytime now."

Francis hugged Sawyer. "See you tomorrow."

He bussed home, replaying the day over and over in his head. They'd met one really weird couple and one really great couple. Tomorrow would be interesting.

• • •

Maria Del Ray vowed to be on time for once, but she forgot to ask the concierge to give her a wake-up call and ended up sleeping in. Not by nature a morning person, she knew she'd have to change her internal clock once she became a parent. She'd do that willingly; she'd do almost anything to hold a baby of her own in her arms. It wasn't fair. Maria had blocked fallopian tubes, a tilted uterus, and had wasted years in a bad relationship; and now, here she was on the downward side of thirty-five and her doctor had given her little chance of conception. She had everything—a lovely home, a career she loved, good friends, family, a lovable dog—everything but a child. Never one to give up, she'd taken matters into her own hands and registered to be on a wait-list for a child. Specifically a baby, although she knew her single status would make that difficult.

When the social worker from Phoenix had called, Maria experienced a glimmer of hope. Now here she was in Vancouver, a lovely city by the sea, racing in a cab to meet the teenagers who held her destiny in their hands.

She'd listened to Ms. Yeung's description of the interview process with a sinking heart. Teenagers were unpredictable, fickle, interesting for sure, but—capable of choosing a mother?

At a quarter past eleven, fifteen minutes late, Maria knocked on Sawyer's front door. Hearing the light tap, Sawyer let out a sigh of relief. "That's her! I was starting to think she got cold feet."

Maria looked much younger than her thirty-seven years. Like Sawyer, she wore leggings and a long shirt. Her short, curly black hair framed a caring face, and her big smile was genuine. "Sorry I'm late," she said breathlessly. "Alarm problems. Gosh, you must be Sawyer!" She embraced Sawyer warmly. "And look at your sweet baby bump."

Sawyer blushed. "Please come in and sit wherever you are comfortable." Introductions were made all round.

Francis asked the first question. "Do you think it will be difficult to raise a child without a father?"

"Not at all. I was raised in a two-parent family, but I'd describe my own mother as distant and my father as emotionally absent. I would be a fully engaged and loving mom, and I've loads of brothers and friends who will provide fun and positive role models. Besides, I've yet to meet the right person, but I will one day, and then, well, I hope he'll love the baby like his own."

Alarm bells went off in Mrs. Martin's head, but her face remained passive. "Dr. Del Ray," she asked, "what made you decide to go the adoption route, instead of…well, you know…"

"I want my child to know that she was loved by her birth parents and by me. There are children who need homes, and I need to be a mother. I don't want to bring another child into the world when so many are waiting for good homes."

Sawyer swallowed. "What sort of school would you send the child to?"

Maria smiled and her face relaxed again. "A private school

and, of course, a university education. But while she's young, she can come to the clinic with me—that's one of the advantages of owning your own business. I'd probably have a nanny. I've got plenty of room at the clinic to set up a small nursery."

"What does your tattoo mean?" Sawyer lifted her own sleeve. "I've got one too. London. It means two things to me—it helps me to remember where I used to live and it's the name of my baby girl."

"Nice. I like the name you've chosen. I love London. I go there at least once every two years. Mine means exactly what it says: *Trust in yourself.* I learned at a very young age that self-confidence leads to self-respect, both of which I would give your child."

Sawyer smiled, happy with the answer.

Maria told them all about her renovated Victorian home in Calgary and her dog, Benny. She chatted on about her parents and her friends in an easy and relaxed manner. She told them how much having a baby would change her life. "Sorry. This means so much to me and I get emotional talking about it."

The interview went on for more than two hours because they felt so comfortable with her, and when she left, they were sad to see her go. "She feels like a big sister," Sawyer noted. "Did you notice that quirky habit she had of scrunching up her nose? I really liked her. She's bubbly and down to earth at the same time!"

"And she looks a bit like you, Sawyer," Francis added. "Plus, she's funny. I loved it when she described pulling that 'stubborn little calf' out of a cow."

Francis and Sawyer both agreed that she'd made it to the finals, but Mrs. Martin seemed more hesitant. "What didn't you like about her, Mom?" Sawyer asked, picking up on her mother's hesitation.

"It's not easy to raise a child on your own. I'd know that more than anyone. In my book, that's a big strike against her."

Francis didn't want to get involved in an argument between Sawyer and her mom; if he had, he would have said, *But Maria has a great career and money. It wouldn't be the same struggle.* Instead, he said, "Let's talk about this as a group. My candidates should be here soon, the last ones. The hardest part of all of this will be choosing."

Mrs. Martin nodded in agreement. Sawyer sighed. "I know."

• • •

Taylor Laberge and Sydney Fox were five minutes early. When they shook hands with Mrs. Martin, they both had strong, confident grips, and she liked them immediately. But it was their daughter who won everyone's hearts.

She bounced into the room, clutching a raggedy, love-worn doll. "Where's the baby?" When she didn't see a baby, her face fell. "I've got a dolly for her. Where is she?"

Taylor scooped her up in his arms and, smiling apologetically at Sawyer, said, "The baby is in her tummy, like you were before you were born. Remember the story about your birth?"

She nodded solemnly, looking directly into his eyes. "Can I tell it?"

"Of course, sweetie."

"I have a mamma and a daddy and a poppa. I'm Star." The little girl's scanned the room, and then she made her way to Jack, who had the afternoon off and who had begged to be present at this interview. She tilted her head and regarded him seriously. "You're the daddy."

He burst out laughing. "I'm not, actually. But it's a common mistake around here." Jack pointed at Francis. "He's the daddy."

Francis blushed, then quickly changed the subject. "Star is an interesting name. How did you get it?"

"Daddy and Poppa wanted a baby more than this," she said, holding her hands out wide. "More than the whole universe. They used to wish on a star for me. 'Twinkle, twinkle, little Star, how we wonder where you are.' They wondered where I was. I was hiding, like your baby is hiding. What's her name?"

"London." Francis look helplessly at Sawyer, who shrugged and rubbed her belly.

"Do you want to touch her?" she asked.

Star extended her small hand and placed it on Sawyer's tummy. "Hello, London," she whispered, her face inches from Sawyer's taut skin.

"She's pretty excited about the possibility of a baby sister," Taylor said. "Please, go ahead and ask us anything you like, and we'll try to get a word in edgewise."

"Well…" Sawyer rubbed the side of her nose. "Do you think it might be hard for Star to suddenly have a sibling to contend with? I mean, she's obviously the center of your world, and that's great, but could it cause problems?"

Sydney glanced at Taylor. "There would be a period of adjustment, and we are prepared for that. We'd be very careful to ensure that Star continues to feel loved and included, while teaching her that we have enough love for both of them."

"Do you think it's hard on Star—the fact that she doesn't have a mother?" Jack asked.

"Uh," Sydney said, "do you mean, can a gay couple be as good parents as a straight couple?"

When Jack opened his mouth to protest, Sydney held up his hand. "It's a fair question. This is what we know: Children need unconditional love, guidance, and some structure. One good parent is a gift, but two committed parents—be they two committed moms or a regular mom and dad or, in our case, two committed dads—are double the gift."

Francis felt a surprising affinity toward the two men. He knew he'd picked well. "If you were chosen, would you like to be at the birth?"

They nodded in unison. "We'd be honored. Will all of you be there?"

"No. Just my mom—she's my coach—and the doctor and the medical staff. Jack and Francis will be in the waiting room."

"Sawyer, if you choose us, your daughter will grow up knowing the sacrifice you made for her, and she'll know how many people cared about her." Taylor's voice broke, and Sydney reached over and patted the back of his hand.

"I'm hugely impressed with you kids." Sydney directed

his next comment at Francis. "It's a brave and very responsible thing you're doing."

"Can you tell us a bit about your lives in Montreal?" Mrs. Martin handed Star a carrot stick. She munched on it contentedly, twirling her hair in her plump fingers.

"We live in a big Victorian house minutes outside the Old Port. Taylor's hours are flexible, so he's home in the mornings. On any afternoons he has a commitment, he'll drop the baby off at our wonderful on-campus daycare, so no nannies. Star is being brought up in both French and English, and the baby would have the same advantage. We have a cabin in the Laurentians, where we spend a month every summer, and in the winter, we spend two weeks somewhere warm. She'll learn to ski, play soccer, go to galleries—have opportunities to discover her own passions."

Taylor said, "The baby will have her own room, next to Star's and across the hall from Sydney and me. When the kids are older, we'd like to get a dog. My two brothers and their families live in Montreal, as do Sydney's mom and dad."

"Do you keep in touch with Star's mom?" Francis asked.

"On her birthday—"

"We eat *la crème glacée* et *les gâteaux* and have a party," interrupted Star. "We write a letter to my mama with my best picture in it. Before I go to sleep, we read her letter and open her present."

As the two hours drew to a close, Taylor, Sydney, and Star had even won the heart of skeptical Sawyer. When they left, nobody said anything. They were all lost in their private thoughts.

Mrs. Martin broke the silence by stating the obvious: "Needless to say, those three made the final round?"

Sawyer smiled. "I didn't think they'd have a chance, but I really liked them."

"Maybe," Jack said hopefully, "if we choose them, I could get to know them a bit better."

"What's the next step?" Francis asked.

Mrs. Martin suggested they invite Kevin to join them and order Chinese. They could discuss the choices and then, if they were all willing, move on to the vote. "That way, we'll have time to think about who we like and why. When we've finished dinner, we can argue for or against our choices. If there is a tie after a show of hands, I'll come in as the tiebreaker. Fair?"

She was about to pick up the phone and order when there was a knock at the door. She opened it to Francis's dad.

"If I know my son," he said, "he's starving, and there hasn't been any time to cook. I've got baby back ribs, coleslaw, fries, an assortment of juices, and chocolate cake."

"Yay!" A chorus of cheers erupted from the living room.

"I'm not staying," Francis's dad explained quickly. "But, Francis, your mom and I are so proud of all of you."

"You're a lucky boy, Francis," Mrs. Martin said after he'd left. "You're clearly the apple of your father's eye!"

Once Kevin had arrived, they attacked the food greedily, and for a while, the only sounds in the room were smacking lips and happy sighs. Only when they'd eaten as much as they could did they turn their attentions back to the difficult task they'd taken on.

Mrs. Martin began. "Maria was lovely, but I don't like the idea of her bringing a strange man into the mix, and she clearly wants a partner eventually. I'd feel so much better if she were a bit more settled. I loved Winston and Michelle, but they live so close to us, and I worry about the idea of running into them with London present. Of course, the Scotts are totally unsuitable."

"I don't agree about Maria," Sawyer said. "You can't hold her single status against her. It doesn't seem fair."

"Maybe not," Jack argued, "but I agree with your mom. Who knows what kind of a man she might end up with? It's too much of a risk."

"Yeah, but we could easily pick a couple, and one of them could divorce, or die, and then the one left behind might remarry," Kevin protested. "Nobody can read the future."

"I'd be more worried about her plan to have a nanny. The nanny would probably spend more time with London than Maria," Francis added. "Why don't we vote on Maria?" Francis had already made up his mind about who he wanted to parent London. He wanted to get on with it.

Mrs. Martin stood up. "Let's begin with Beth and David Scott from Kelowna."

Kevin groaned.

"What a disaster they were," Sawyer said.

"All the same, show of hands *for* the Scotts." Mrs. Martin nodded as she looked at the others. "As we thought. Show of hands *against* the Scotts." All four of them put both their hands up. "That was quick and easy." Mrs. Martin laughed. Now we can move on to a show of hands for Maria."

Sawyer's hand shot up. Kevin's followed. "Okay." Mrs. Martin paused. "Show of hands against Maria Del Ray from Alberta."

Francis waved his hand above his head. They all looked at Jack. "You can't be undecided," Sawyer told him. "You have to make up your mind."

"I'm not undecided," Jack said. "I like her, and maybe it's not fair, but life isn't fair." He raised his hand. "That's a tie."

All eyes went to Mrs. Martin. Nobody envied her role as tiebreaker. She took only a few moments to consider what to do before she spoke up. "I'm sorry, Sawyer, but I'm not willing to take the chance on her future choice of a boyfriend or husband. Fair or not fair. Besides, I think she's got too much to juggle in her busy life." Mrs. Martin raised her hand. "Maria's out. It's sad, but we have to put the baby first, and that's what I'm doing."

"Who's going to tell her the bad news?"

"Don't worry, Kevin. Ms. Yeung from Phoenix will take care of that. Now what about our third couple? Winston and Michelle Oliver from Vancouver?"

Jack spoke up. "Well, I really liked them, and not only because I picked them. However, now that I think about it, I agree with Mrs. Martin. They live in the same city as we do. It's too close. I mean, the chances are really good that any one of us could run into them. I kind of wish I'd thought of that earlier, before we got their hopes up."

"I don't think that should matter," Kevin protested.

"They were really great," Sawyer said. "I'm confident they'd be equally fantastic parents. When London's old enough to look up her parents, she'll be close by and we can all get to know her better. What do you think, Francis?"

"They were cool. I'm not sure. I mean, except for the Scotts, they were all wonderful people. This is so hard."

"Well, let's vote." Mrs. Martin said. "I agree with Francis. This isn't easy at all. A show of hands for Winston and Michelle."

"They get my vote." Jack raised his hand.

Kevin also raised his hand. "Mine too."

"So we can assume this is another tie?" Mrs. Martin sighed. "I didn't expect to be in this position twice. How about if we deal with this after we've voted on the Fox-Laberge couple? Maria and the Scotts are out, and it's a tie with the Olivers. So, on to Taylor and Sydney and Star."

Francis's hand shot up, followed by Sawyer's and Jack's. "I can't vote against them. They are perfect. I wish they were my parents."

"Yeah." Kevin's hand went up. "London Laberge-Fox it is!"

Mrs. Martin hugged her daughter. "I would have voted for them too! I think they will be fabulous parents for London." She checked her watch. "I think I'll give Ms. Yeung a quick call. I know she's very curious to learn who we have chosen."

"Speaker phone," Sawyer demanded. "We all want to hear what she says."

Seconds later, they got their wish. "I'm not supposed to say this," Ms. Yeung bubbled, "but I'm thrilled with your choice.

They are genuine, lovely people. As soon as the rest of the paperwork is completed I'll call and let them know." She lowered her voice. "I'm looking forward to that call as much as I'm dreading the others."

Chapter Nineteen

By the end of your ninth month, your baby is
settling into the fetal position, upside down
with her head against the birth canal, legs
tucked up to chest, and knees against nose.
The bones of baby's head are soft and flexible
to ease the process of delivery through the
birth canal.

Excerpt: *From Conception to Birth*

Less than a week later, Ms. Yeung found herself with Sawyer
and her mother, seated in their cozy living room, sipping tea.
Before them lay a stack of legal documents Ms Yeung wanted
them to review. It had taken a long time and much effort to
arrive at this place, but they'd done it.

"Francis should be here any minute," Sawyer promised.

Her huge belly meant that sitting in one position for too long caused great discomfort. As if on cue, a rap on the door announced Francis's arrival. "Sorry I'm late," he apologized. "Stupid bus."

"Don't worry about it. Mint tea?"

Francis didn't really like herbal tea, but he didn't want to be rude. "Thank you, Mrs. Martin."

"Sawyer really misses her coffee, but I keep telling her that she'll be back on the java soon enough."

I could use some java, Francis thought to himself.

"I can't wait for my first taste," Sawyer confirmed with a smile. "Maybe I'll splurge on a latte. It's good to have some things to look forward to after…well, after the birth…"

Ms. Yeung sipped her tea. "This is delicious." She cleared her throat. She'd been in many similar situations, but had seldom witnessed Sawyer's composure and dignity, or her mother's loyal support, and to have the young dad present was almost unheard of. "Of course, initially, Francis, you too will be on the birth certificate, until the parents apply to change that, so the adoption will require both of your signatures."

Ms. Yeung flashed her brightest smile. "I just want to reiterate a few important points. As we discussed earlier, you'll have seven days from the date of the child's birth to sign the adoption papers. You will still have twenty-one days after signing the papers to change your mind. I sincerely hope neither of you will exercise that option, but it's there if you need to. Realize that doing so is a heartbreak for everyone, but especially for the adoptive parents."

"Don't worry," Sawyer reassured her. "That's not going to happen. I know this is the best thing for London." She turned to Francis. "Right?"

He nodded, but with nothing to say, kept quiet, studying Ms. Yeung. He could tell she had a great deal of admiration for Sawyer, but she was sharp and didn't miss a thing, not even the sadness that often clouded Sawyer's eyes as the birth drew nearer. Ms. Yeung nodded. "You're doing a wonderful thing," she said softly.

Sawyer blinked several times. "I know, but it doesn't always feel that way."

Ms. Yeung patted Sawyer's knee. "I've arranged for you to meet with our lawyers to actually sign all the papers. Because Sawyer's under eighteen," she said, turning to Sawyer's mom, "you will also need to be present."

"Of course." She closed her hand over her daughter's. "We're in this together."

"Would you be willing to tell me how you came to your decision? Do either of you have any doubts about Taylor and Sydney, before I inform them?"

Sawyer glanced at her mother, who simply nodded her head. "Go on, sweetheart. Tell her what you thought of all of the couples."

"Well," Sawyer began, "Beth and David didn't even make it to first base. I'd feel sorry for any child unlucky enough to end up in their home. I don't know how they even got through your screening process. Those two are miserable, especially David."

"It blew me away." Francis frowned. "They weren't anything like I thought they'd be. Definitely check them out again."

"We will," assured Ms. Yeung. "They passed the home test and had great reference letters, but that was some time ago. I'll spend a little more time with them. I think this process has taken its toll on them in the interim years. Not all couples make it. They were solid when they did the home study, but now...who knows? It's not easy." She switched course. "What about Maria?"

Sawyer's mother shuffled uncomfortably in her chair. "The kids loved Maria, but I had my doubts. I've been a single mom since Sawyer's dad left us. Honestly, it hasn't been easy. Besides, I think Maria wants a partner, and finding one gets harder when you're a mother. Trust me, I know. But I guess none of us can see the future, and couples are vulnerable to unforeseen events too—good and bad."

"I liked Maria," Sawyer interrupted, "but she got voted out. I still think she'd be a great mom, but we all agreed that we each had an equal vote, and Maria lost out."

"I thought she was lovely too," Ms. Yeung agreed. She'd secretly been hoping they'd choose the accomplished single mom, but experience had taught her that this would be unlikely. "But not to worry. I'll continue to work hard on her behalf. And Winston and Michelle?"

"We all loved them," Sawyer enthused. "The only reason we didn't think they'd work out was because they live so close."

"We didn't want to run into them unexpectedly, especially

if they had London with them," Francis added. "That would be awkward, to say the least."

"That's a really good point," Ms. Yeung agreed. "And you are correct. They are wonderful people, and there are three other out-of-town pregnant women interested in meeting them. They'll be parents soon enough."

Sawyer's mother breathed a sigh of relief. "I'm very pleased to hear that."

"Taylor and Sydney already have a child," Sawyer said, "but they were the perfect couple and we all feel good about them."

"That's the most important thing." Ms. Yeung stood up. "Now that I'm convinced that you're one hundred percent comfortable with your choice, I'll go back to my office and make the phone calls. I want to assure you that I'm as enthusiastic about the Fox-Laberge choice as you are."

Sawyer's face lit up. Francis struggled not to pump the air with his fist. He'd known from the very start that they were the right couple, and now it had been confirmed.

After Ms. Yeung left, Francis stayed for a short time before Sawyer said she needed a rest. Once alone in her bedroom, she lay down on her bed and pulled the covers up over her face. She'd been tired lately, finding it more difficult to move around. This would be her last week at school. She'd do her best to finish the year online, but it was a challenge to concentrate. With the baby's future decided, she felt a great weight lifted. Because she knew that London could hear and feel her, Sawyer would be positive, no matter how hard that might be.

• • •

Ms. Yeung sat down at her desk and picked up her phone. She had four calls to make. Two would be heartbreaking, one difficult, and one would remind her of why she loved her work so much. Of course, she saved the best for last.

When the phone rang in the Scotts' house, Beth saw Phoenix's number on the call display and picked up halfway through the second ring. "Hello! I hope this is good news." She crossed herself.

"I'm sorry," Ms. Yeung responded quickly. "But I'm afraid you and your husband are still on the list." She could picture the scene in the Scott household and regretted the pain she had inflicted on them.

David Scott saw his wife's face crumple and his heart sank. Their nightmare would continue. After Beth hung up, he tried to comfort her, but she pushed him away.

"Leave me alone," she said flatly.

"I'm not sure we love each other enough to raise a child together right now," David said, wondering if they'd survive as a couple through another round.

Maria had just finished examining a colicky horse when her cell phone buzzed. "Hello," she answered, full of hope. "Dr. Del Ray."

"Hello, Maria. It's—"

"I know who it is," Maria said. "And I can tell by your tone, it's not good news." She kept her voice strong while her heart broke.

"I know how hard this is," Ms. Yeung said sympathetically. "But we *are* going to find a match soon, Maria. I really think we should talk about an international adoption, again. It's a bit of a wait, but as I've said before, it's a better option for single applicants. The children are in orphanages, and you'd be matched up with a child by our people on the ground. Let's talk again once you've had a chance to get over this."

The third call wasn't any easier. Frankly, she'd been surprised when Sawyer hadn't named Michelle and Winston as the baby's parents, but she'd appreciated that proximity could be a very real issue.

Michelle answered the phone. "Hang on a sec," she said breathlessly. "I'm going to put you on speaker so Winston can hear everything."

"I'm sorry, Michelle and Winston, but it's not good news." Ms. Yeung gave them a moment to reply. When they didn't, she continued. "Don't lose heart. The only difficulty was that you lived close by. It won't be terribly difficult for me to find you a child. Please be patient. I already have two other babies in mind where proximity won't be an issue. A third one is an open adoption, for which being nearby isn't a liability. This time it just wasn't meant to be."

After they'd hung up, Michelle and Winston went for a long walk on the beach. "It's going to okay," Winston whispered to Michelle. "We have to do what Ms. Yeung advises. We have to be patient for a little while longer."

At last, Ms. Yeung made the call she'd been looking forward to. Taylor ran for the phone, but he hesitated when he saw the number. Finally, on the third ring, he answered with a tentative "*Allo?*"

He and Sydney wanted a second child so badly, but they realized it would take special people to accept them. Special people, they both knew, were few and far between. "Good news, I hope?"

Sydney stood at his elbow, Star in his arms. He kept his eyes glued on Taylor, watching his facial expressions for clues. When the tears started down Taylor's cheeks, his heart sank. He hugged Star closer.

"Thank you, Ms. Yeung." Taylor dropped the phone gently into its base. "Sydney," he said in a shaky voice, "it looks like we'll be returning to Vancouver in a couple of weeks."

Sydney, for once, was speechless. "*Tu es sûr?*"

"*Oui, sans aucun doute.*" Taylor grinned. "*Nous sommes vraiment bénis.*"

"Why are we blessed, Dad?" Star wanted to know.

Sydney pulled Taylor into his embrace. "Because we are going to be parents for a second time. You're going to have a baby sister."

Star clapped her hands together. "*Une soeur!*"

• • •

Both Francis and Kevin visited Sawyer regularly, even during their exams. At first Kevin went because he couldn't stand to be at home where the vacuum created by his father's death threatened to suffocate him. Then he went because he felt welcome and part of something bigger than himself.

Whenever Francis went, his mother sent packages of goodies. One cool, sunny May afternoon, the boys showed up together. Francis had a large box of truffles in his satchel.

They found Sawyer at the kitchen table and Jack leaning out the window smoking. "For the baby's health," he explained.

"I'm going to get fat," Sawyer lamented, tearing open the box. "No wonder I can't see my toes anymore!" She quickly popped three truffles into her mouth.

"Well, you *are* nine months pregnant. Soon you'll be your old skinny self again." Francis helped himself to a truffle.

"Do you think your mom will keep sending over treats after the baby is born? I'm spoiled now."

"What are we celebrating?" Kevin asked.

"Well, for one thing, today everything about the baby is settled." Sawyer clapped her hands. "It's about time too. It hurts to walk. And I can't focus on anything. I'm hungry all the time." She picked up another chocolate. "I can't believe I'm eating truffles now. The kids in my class sent over a box of macaroons yesterday. They said they're going to have a class party when the baby is born."

"Well, you're eating for two." Kevin laughed. "That's crazy about the kids in your class. We don't talk about it at school, even though word's leaked out. Kids shoot Francis weird looks. Right, Francis? But that's about it."

"Don't get any ideas," Francis teased. "No party for me."

Sawyer frowned at him. "It's hardly a secret. I mean, I'm not ashamed. Besides, look at me."

"That's not what I meant. I think it's cool how open you are. I just meant, a party…"

"Kevin had a party when he lost his dad. You called it a wake. A party is a way of acknowledging someone or some occasion, like a birth or a death or a baby—it's still an occasion." Sawyer sounded exasperated. "The party they had for me on my last day of school wasn't a shower or anything. They were really clear about that. They didn't give me baby gifts. They gave me books and earrings and—wait till you see what they made me." She pushed herself out of her chair and waddled into her bedroom, returning with a giant card that she handed to Francis. "Check this out," she said, obviously pleased.

Elegant calligraphy covered the surface. "It's a letter," he said. "Dear Sawyer," he read. "We are so lucky to have you in our class. We have watched you face a tough situation with honesty and dignity. You have thirty friends in this class, so you're not the 'new girl' anymore. You are one of us. We are here for you. Good luck!" Francis studied it before passing it to Kevin. "Look, they've all signed it, including the teacher, Miss Addison."

"I know," Sawyer crowed. "You know what this means, right?"

"It means you don't need us anymore," said Kevin.

Sawyer laughed. "No, you idiot. I'll always need you guys. But they like me, despite everything. That's how it was in London. That's what I missed the most when we moved. I felt so lonely in school here, but not now. Finally, this place feels like home."

Jack, who'd been quietly listening to the conversation, spoke up. "That's what I've been trying to tell you all along. Home isn't a place. It's where the people who love you are."

"I know, Jack. It's taken a while, but I get it."

"You know," Kevin said later, as he and Francis waited for the bus. "Sawyer is a pretty amazing person."

"Yeah," Francis agreed. "I feel like so much has happened since we met at that dance…" His voice trailed off. "Hard stuff, like your dad, and then she got pregnant. But—"

Kevin finished the sentence for him. "But somehow good has come out of it. My dad always said life works that way, but up until now, I never really believed it."

Chapter Twenty

If ever there is tomorrow when we're not
together…there is something you must
always remember. You are braver than you
believe, stronger than you seem, and smarter
than you think. But the most important thing
is, even if we're apart…I'll always be with you.
Excerpt: Sawyer Martin's diary, quoting A.A. Milne

On May 12, Taylor and Sydney had flown to Vancouver and taken a suite in a hotel near the British Columbia Women's Hospital. Even though the baby wasn't due for two weeks, they didn't want to risk missing her birthday.

A week before her due date, Sawyer was strolling down Main Street with Jack. Jack slowed his pace to match Sawyer's. Even though she'd been experiencing uncomfortable pressure in her pelvis, she insisted on going out. "I'm restless." The air had lost its bite, and the warm sunshine promised longer days. Sawyer, thirty pounds heavier, moved slowly.

She was tired and cranky. "I'm really craving a chocolate milk," she announced.

They slipped into Joe's convenience store, and while Jack browsed the magazines, Sawyer went in search of her drink. When Jack heard a startled cry, he rushed to the cooler and discovered Sawyer standing in a pool of water. "Help," she cried.

"Did something break?"

"Yeah, Jack. You could say that. It's my water."

His brow creased. "Huh?"

"My water broke. As in, the baby is on her way."

"But it's a week early! It can't be today." Jack pulled his phone out of his pocket. "Should I call 911?"

"No. Call my mom. Tell her to meet us at the hospital. I'm okay. Just a little cramping."

"Are you sure?"

"Is there anything I can do for you?" Joe came out from behind the counter. "Would you like to sit down?"

"I'm just sorry about the mess." Sawyer grimaced. "Let's go, Jack. *Now!*"

She waddled at high speed out of the store. Jack followed her, still clutching his phone.

Less than half an hour later, a young nurse ushered Sawyer into a birthing suite. "It's your lucky day," she said with a smile. "We're not full at all. You'll get lots of attention." She turned to Jack. "You'll have to wait outside."

"Jack is one of my birth partners," Sawyer told her.

Jack nodded. "I'd kind of like to sit down."

"Thank god there are more partners." Sawyer sighed. "Jack, call Francis. He'll get Kevin. Make sure you call the dads. Do it before you faint."

"Oh, yeah." He rushed out of the room, dialing numbers frantically on his phone.

"Did you say dads with an *s*?" the nurse queried.

"It's a long story," Sawyer began. "You see—" Her first really strong contraction hit her, and she doubled over in pain.

Outside the room, Jack heard her cry out and his legs turned to spaghetti. *Hurry up, guys. I can't do this alone.*

Sydney and Taylor were the first to arrive, followed by Sawyer's mother. Francis, Kevin, and Francis's parents were close behind. They all hurried into the birthing suite to check on Sawyer.

"It's awfully crowded in here," the maternity nurse pointed out good-naturedly.

"Yes," said Sawyer. Her eyes sought out Taylor and Sydney. "Where's Star?"

"We left her with friends. She'll come after the baby is born." Taylor took her hand and squeezed it.

"Good luck, Sawyer," Francis said. "We'll be right outside if you need us."

To his surprise, his mother bent over and kissed Sawyer on the cheek. "You're a lovely, brave girl," she said gently in her ear. His dad put his arm around his wife. "I second that," he added. "We'll be here the whole time." They left the labor suite holding hands. Francis felt a rush of love toward them.

"Come on." Kevin took his arm. "We have to go outside too. Good luck, Sawyer." She let out a long breath and turned to them. "This is it."

Francis stood awkwardly, not moving until Kevin guided him from the room.

Dr. Chung arrived minutes later to find Mrs. Martin, Sydney, and Taylor gathered around her patient, the three of them encouraging her with every contraction. A quick examination showed her to be six centimeters dilated. "Things are moving quickly," she reassured Sawyer. "It's probably too late for an epidural, but I can offer you some of that laughing gas we talked about to help ease your anxiety."

Sawyer accepted gratefully. The contractions were closer now, and the pain threatened to overwhelm her. "Mom," she cried out. "It hurts too much. I can't do this."

"Oh, yes you can, sweetie." Her mother pressed a cold cloth to her daughter's damp forehead. "I love you, and you can do this."

Sawyer smiled before moaning through another stronger contraction.

Two hours later, Dr. Chung checked her again. "You're almost there! It's time to start pushing."

Twenty minutes later, Sawyer gave birth to an eight-pound baby girl. London Sawyer Fox-Laberge entered the world under the adoring eyes of her birth family and her adoptive family.

When Francis, his parents, Jack, and Kevin filed into the suite, Sawyer was sitting up in bed sipping on a glass of apple juice. "I'm starving," she declared. "That was hard work."

Beside her, swaddled in a pink blanket, Baby London slept peacefully. "She's beautiful," murmured Francis's mother. She touched the baby's cheek. The baby stirred and blinked her eyes open. "Beautiful little London." She choked back tears. Seeing her anguish, Taylor wrapped his arms around her.

"Your London will be loved and looked after all of her life. That is my promise to you and to your family."

Francis's mom blinked back tears. "Thank you. That means so much to me—to us." She turned to Sawyer. "She's a beautiful baby. Absolutely lovely. Perfect."

His dad bent over London. He placed a kiss on her head. "She certainly is," he agreed. He took a step back, changed his mind, and glanced at the baby once again. He reached out and wrapped his large hand around her tiny one, murmuring something inaudible to her. When he turned away, his face was a mask. "Francis," he said, his voice wavering. "Your mother and I have said our good-byes. We'll wait outside for you, if you like."

"That's okay," Francis answered. "I'll make my own way home." Only after they'd left did he turn to face the swaddled form in the crib. "She's so small," he observed, his voice full of wonder. The baby's eyes opened. Big, clear blue eyes, and she let out a tiny cry.

Mrs. Martin touched him on the shoulder. "Would you like to hold her?"

"Not really," Francis said. "She looks so fragile. But she's got a head of hair."

"She's more resilient than you might think." Mrs. Martin

gave him an encouraging smile. "Look, her little fingers are moving."

Francis took London in his arms, marveling at her miniature perfection. He held her only for a few minutes. "Hello, London," he whispered. "I'll write to you. I promise."

Feeling an unexpected wave of emotion, he handed the baby to Sydney. "Take good care of her." His voice cracked. Taylor wrapped a sympathetic arm around his shoulder.

Jack held London next. He rocked her back and forth rhythmically. He told her how lucky she was. He breathed in her smell and then he gave her back to the nurse.

"Would you like to feed her?"

"Maybe once. Later. When it's just us," Sawyer said sadly.

Sydney and Taylor had been watching Jack's interaction with their baby closely. They waited until the others were gathered around London and Sawyer, then they took him aside. "Sawyer's mother has told us how supportive you've been and what a good friend you are to her daughter," Taylor said.

"She's my best friend," Jack replied simply.

Taylor nodded. "If you ever need anybody to talk to, here's our email. You've done so much for us. We'd like to return the favor."

Sawyer spent that night with London. The nurse gave Sawyer drugs to dry up her milk, and London took to her bottle lustily. Sawyer did change her diapers and she cuddled her, only giving her up to the nurses reluctantly when she couldn't stay awake any longer. She memorized London's tiny fingers, perfect toes, and the shape of her clear blue eyes and precious little nose.

She breathed in her baby's scent and shed more than a few private tears, but this was her time with her baby and she refused to ruin it by crying the night away. In her heart she still knew she was doing the best thing for London. That didn't take away her sadness, but it did make her feel proud of herself and grateful for her friends and for London's dads.

Twenty-four hours later, she placed Baby London into the arms of her adoptive parents, Taylor and Sydney. Star gazed at her new baby sister, wide-eyed. "I love you, London," she said and planted a gentle kiss on her forehead. "Thank you, Sawyer, for our baby."

Taylor took Sydney's hand. He'd promised himself he wouldn't cry, but they owed this young girl so much. "Thank you," he said softly.

Sawyer managed a weak smile. "I knew that saying good-bye to London would be difficult, but you've made it so much easier."

Before they left, they gave Sawyer a small silver heart locket on a lacy chain. She turned it over. *London* was engraved on the back. Inside she discovered a tiny picture of her daughter.

She didn't cry in front of the others, not once. Francis did, though, as did Kevin and Jack. "How can you be so stoic?" Jack inquired.

"London has not one but two amazing dads and a sister. It's the best thing I could give her. What's to cry about? Besides," she said, pulling down the neck of her shirt, "her name is tattooed on my shoulder. London will always be with me."

Epilogue

Every so often, I reread the copy of my letter to my daughter. Sometimes it makes me cry. It surprises me how much I love her, even though I don't know her at all.

I'm not going to read you the letter. It's just between the two of us, but I will share a bit.

I wrote about myself because I want London to know all about me—the real me. I tried to think of what I would want to know if I were in her shoes. I told her the kind of music I like and the sports I play, the name of my favorite superhero, the title of my most loved book. I told her that family and friends are the most important things in life. I said doing the right thing does not always mean doing the easiest thing.

I told her how much her mom and I loved her.

I stuck a photo of all of us—myself, Kevin, Jack, and Sawyer—into the envelope with the letter: On the envelope I wrote: *To London Fox-Laberge @ eighteen years old.*

I sealed the letter and sent it off to Ms. Yeung.

It took a long time for everyone to come around and stop being sad about saying good-bye to London, but in the end, I am proud of how we handled ourselves.

My mom made some quips about birth control, but I told her that I'd learned my lesson! It's true. And the lesson I learned? I was as responsible as Sawyer for creating London.

Last year is behind us now, and we are all moving on. Sawyer will graduate with honors. Jack lives above the coffee shop where he still works part-time while going to university and getting top marks. He's doing his B.Sc with a major in Computer Science. He'll ace it. He has a really nice boyfriend. He has stayed in contact with London's parents, but that's between them.

Kevin will always miss his dad, but their kind of relationship is stronger than death.

My mom will always hold London close to her heart, and it's the same for my dad. We don't talk about it, but we all think about that perfect baby girl.

And me? I am looking forward to grade eleven next fall. I've been picked for the City soccer team and I'm pumped about that.

If Mr. Croyden were here, I'd tell him this: I've kept my promise. I talk to Kevin about him all the time. I tell him that his father's greatest accomplishment was being a dad. And I try to live well, like he asked me to. I think I finally understand what he meant when he told me to "be the right kind of man."

So, you could say that life is back to normal, but never a day goes by that I don't think about my daughter, and I hope that never changes. More than that, I hope one day, when she is grown up, she'll read my letter and she'll know that we did what we did out of love.

Acknowledgments

I'd like to thank the following people for their comments, thoughts, encouragement and inspiration:

My friend, coach and cheerleader, Joy Gugeler for her steadfast belief in me.

My beta readers for their insightful observations and suggestions:

Natalie Gates, Maya Pozzolo, Brittany G, Leslie-Ann Paige, Jessica Wilson, Catherine Charlebois, Janelle Armstrong, Molly Barneau, Clarice Lundeau, and Clayton Bambrough.

Special thanks also to Stiwido Maelor, the International Writers' Residency in Corris, Wales, for the precious gift of solitude and time that allowed me to dedicate weeks to the process of writing a novel.

I am very grateful to my publisher, Second Story Press,

and my skilled editor, Kathryn Cole, for their dedication to this novel and for putting it into the hands of readers.

Huge thanks also to the Vancouver chapter of Shut Up and Write for making writing a quiet, yet extraordinary social experience.

And finally, thank you to my family for your grace in walking this path with me yet again.

About the Author

JULIE BURTINSHAW is an award-winning author of novels for young adults, including *The Darkness Between the Stars, The Perfect Cut, The Freedom of Jenny, Adrift,* and *Dead Reckoning.* Julie writes with young people in mind because she insists on asking "why?" and so do they. She believes her readers face challenges with hope, and hardship with optimism. They are fighting to find their way in life—just like the characters in her books. Julie teaches writers' workshops in high schools across Canada and lives in Vancouver, British Columbia. She is active on social media and encourages readers to contact her with questions and comments. You can find her on Facebook and follow her on Twitter @WriterJulie.